I0600686

Dreams

by Tom Sharkey

A SAMUEL FRENCH ACTING EDITION

SAMUEL FRENCH

FOUNDED 1830

SAMUELFRENCH.COM

ISBN 978-0-573-70010-1   Printed in U.S.A.   #28119

MUSIC USE NOTE

Licensees are solely responsible for obtaining formal written permission from copyright owners to use copyrighted music in the performance of this play and are strongly cautioned to do so. If no such permission is obtained by the licensee, then the licensee must use only original music that the licensee owns and controls. Licensees are solely responsible and liable for all music clearances and shall indemnify the copyright owners of the play and their licensing agent, Samuel French, Inc., against any costs, expenses, losses and liabilities arising from the use of music by licensees.

IMPORTANT BILLING AND CREDIT REQUIREMENTS

All producers of *DREAMS must* give credit to the Author of the Play in all programs distributed in connection with performances of the Play, and in all instances in which the title of the Play appears for the purposes of advertising, publicizing or otherwise exploiting the Play and/or a production. The name of the Author *must* appear on a separate line on which no other name appears, immediately following the title and *must* appear in size of type not less than fifty percent of the size of the title type.

CHARACTERS

Since there are two dreams – or two realities? – the lead character, **DAVID**, is played by two actors. The other ten characters appear in only one "dream" or the other and are played by five actors, the pairings indicating the double roles.

DAVID TAGGART – an ex-drug user, a dreamer.

DAVID ROSS – an attorney, a dreamer.

Actor 1 (Female) plays:

MEREDITH – Taggart's sister.

FRAN – Ross's wife.

Actor 2 (Hispanic Male) plays:

PEPITO – Taggart's best friend, also an ex-drug user.

JACK – Ross's best friend, an attorney.

Actor 3 (Female) plays:

ANITA – Taggart's mistress.

BECKY – Ross's secretary.

Actor 4 (Male) plays:

SLIGO – a rogue policeman.

PEMBERTON – a psychiatrist.

Actor 5 (Black Male) plays:

BLACKMAN – a drug pusher.

CHARLIE BISHOP – an attorney.

SETTING

The time is the present.

The stage is divided by lighting and platforms into six playing areas, some of which may overlap.

Upstage right is the Ross bedroom: a double bed with a night table and lamp.

Upstage center is the Ross kitchen: a table, chairs and perhaps a background of cabinets.

Upstage left is the bar scene: largely a table and two chairs.

Downstage right is the office scene: a desk, a telephone, an intercom, and two chairs which, by re-angling the furniture, will denote three different offices.

Downstage center is an empty area which is used for the pure "nightmare" of the opening scene and for the street scene later on.

Downstage left is a second bedroom. It holds a bed with a nondescript quilt when the room is Meredith's; a night table is added, the bed is re-angled, and the quilt is removed to reveal a lavender sheet when the room is Anita's; finally, a telephone is added to the night table and the sheet is replaced by a rough wool blanket to convert the scene to a cheap hotel room.

ACT ONE

(AT RISE: the stage is in darkness. We hear a siren's wail, a police whistle, and muffled shouts of, "There he goes!" and, "Head him off!" as the stage is raked with spotlights. DAVID TAGGART, about 30, enters left, out of breath, frightened, and seeking to escape. He pauses downstage center, the sounds falling to silence and the spotlights holding him.)

TAGGART. *(desperate)* Got to get away, got to get away. *(starts upstage right)*

FIRST VOICE. Not this way, Ace.

SECOND VOICE. *(as* **TAGGART** *changes direction)* I wouldn't try it.

THIRD VOICE – SLIGO. *(as* **TAGGART** *again changes directions, a soft but oddly menacing brogue:)* It seems we have you in a box, Davey-boy.

TAGGART. *(freezes, tries to shield his eyes against the lights)* Who are you? What do you want?

FIRST VOICE. *(heavy sarcasm)* We serve, Taggart.

SECOND VOICE. *(overlapping)* And protect!

SLIGO. *(overlapping)* They sometimes call us the Thin Blue Line.

TAGGART. *(doubtful)* Police? I can't see you.

SLIGO. Come on, Davey. Be a good lad and tell us where the parcel is.

TAGGART. What parcel?

FIRST VOICE. *(simultaneous)* Don't say what parcel! *(then)* He said it.

SECOND VOICE. We can drop you right where you stand.

TAGGART. I don't know what you're talking about.

SLIGO. Davey, you were down on the street just now. You saw one of our fellow officers pushed through a plate glass window.

FIRST VOICE. Saw it? Maybe he did the pushing.

TAGGART. *(shouts at* **FIRST VOICE***)* I DIDN'T!

SLIGO. He was after it, Davey. He was in pursuit of the man who had it.

SECOND VOICE. Where did the man go?

FIRST VOICE. Where did he drop it?

TAGGART. I saw a commotion…I ran.

SLIGO. Where did the fellow drop it, lad?

TAGGART. I don't know. I ran. I'm clean.

SECOND VOICE. You're a junky, Taggart.

TAGGART. I'm clean! I'm clean a year.

FIRST VOICE. Sligo, this ain't making it.

SLIGO. *(sighs)* I know, I know.

SECOND VOICE. We got to make it, Sligo.

SLIGO. As usual, you boys are right. Be good enough to kill the lights, will you?

TAGGART. *(backing)* What are you going to do?

FIRST VOICE. *(relays the command)* Kill the lights!

(Lights fall to near-black as **TAGGART** *is approached by three shadowy figures.)*

TAGGART. Hey, don't.

SLIGO. Hold the lad. Steady now.

TAGGART. *(reacts to being hit)* Oh! Please.

SLIGO. Hold him good and tight.

TAGGART. *(a sustained scream)* AGHHH!

(Lights fall to black.)

(a desperate plea) God…somebody…help me!

LITTLE GIRL'S VOICE. *(frightened)* Mommy! Mommy!

(Lights come up in the Ross Bedroom. FRAN ROSS, a handsome woman of about 30 who wears a robe over her nightgown, stands at the table, having just turned the lamp on. DAVID ROSS, also about 30 and resembling DAVID TAGGART physically, is sitting on the edge of the bed, scared, and staring blankly into space.)

FRAN. David...are you all right?

(There is no response. She touches his shoulder.)

ROSS. *(recoils from the unexpected touch, frightened)* Aagh – Aagh – *Aagh!*

(The growing intensity of his fear peaks as his eyes at last focus on FRAN. Then his mind seems to shift from fantasy to reality, his fear a gripping memory.)

Fran...? What's going on? What happened?

FRAN. You were dreaming.

ROSS. I heard...a child.

FRAN. *(nods)* Maureen. Peggy convinced her the way to stop dreaming was to wear rollerskates to bed. *(shows him a child's strap-and-buckle rollerskate)*

ROSS. Rollerskates?

FRAN. One got twisted around her ankle. She thought someone had hold of her and wouldn't let go. *(sighing)* I barely got her back to sleep when *you* started.

ROSS. *(as feelings of relief wash over him)* Wow. Nightmare.

FRAN. *(nervous)* You frightened me. For a minute I couldn't wake you.

ROSS. It was so real. Policemen...beating me...an abandoned building. They said I had a parcel.

FRAN. What sort of parcel?

ROSS. I don't know. Drugs maybe. I thought they were honest to God going to kill me. *(moves away from her)* I'd better take something, a sleeping pill, a tranquilizer.

FRAN. You took two Seconals before you went to bed.

ROSS. *(surprise)* Aren't they supposed to *keep* you from dreaming?

FRAN. *(brightly)* Next time try rollerskates. *(as he glowers at her)* Sorry.

ROSS. *(after a moment)* Do we know anyone named Taggart?

FRAN. No…

ROSS. That's what they called me in the dream: David Taggart. I don't know why, it seemed to fit. I never questioned it.

FRAN. Honey…come back to bed, ha?

ROSS. *(whirls on her)* Don't talk to me like that! I'm not one of your children!

FRAN. *(defensive)* I was not talking to you like you were one of my children.

ROSS. Then *what?*

FRAN. I don't know. My little brother, maybe.

ROSS. *(disgusted)* Cut it out.

FRAN. *(watches him a moment)* David…sit beside me. Tell you the truth, I'm still a little frightened.

ROSS. *(recovers his composure, goes to her)* I'm sorry.

FRAN. *(touches him)* Why don't you lie down? Turn the lights out? I'll make it worth your while.

ROSS. Will you…put that in writing?

FRAN. I did. Ten years ago next month. Don't you remember?

ROSS. I was there, wasn't I? *(kisses her)*

FRAN. *(as lights start down)* David-love – David!

*(Lights fall completely in Ross Bedroom. Come up in Meredith's Room. **TAGGART** lies supine on a cot. **PEPITO**, a Mexican-American of about **TAGGART**'s age, stands at his side.)*

PEPITO. *(as in mid-conversation)* …Because I can *see* you're awake! David, my friend, open your eyes.

TAGGART. *(comes fully awake, frightened)* Huhhh?

PEPITO. *(reassuring)* You're all right, David. You're safe now.

TAGGART. *(tries to rise)* Who?…What?

PEPITO. Do not disturb yourself. Your belly will ache for a time. They did a good job on you.

TAGGART. *(a sudden severe pain)* My head – !

PEPITO. *(examines top of* **TAGGART***'s head)* Yes. They gave you a good shot there. You are fortunate to be alive, my friend. The child's scream is what saved you.

LITTLE GIRL'S VOICE. *(as before)* Mommy! Mommy!

TAGGART. *(disoriented)* Child?

WOMAN'S VOICE. *(the eternal mother)* I told you to get in the house!

PEPITO. *(explains)* A little girl. She and her sister were at play in the abandoned building. They saw what the policemen did. Finally she could stand it no longer. She cried out. She and her sister ran. *(shrugs with humor)* The policemen ran too.

*(***TAGGART*** stares hard at him, the fantasy at last seeming to flee his mind, reality to return.)*

TAGGART. Pepito!

PEPITO. Ah, you know me at last. No, don't get up. Rest, David. I was afraid I might lose you.

TAGGART. *(takes in his surroundings)* What *is* this place?

PEPITO. Your sister's apartment. I had to take you somewhere. Sligo and his compadres will be all over the Halfway House by now.

TAGGART. *(as it becomes clearer and clearer)* You're Pepito. I'm…David Taggart.

PEPITO. We live at the Halfway House.

TAGGART. Second Avenue. We're…drug users.

PEPITO. *(laughs)* Ex-drug users. An important distinction. Rest now. Do not disturb yourself.

TAGGART. Pepito…I had the screwiest dream.

PEPITO. A user of drugs has many dreams. Long after he has stopped, they are with him.

TAGGART. It was so damn real!

PEPITO. As are mine. Did I tell you? In Arizona I lived in a colony, we ate peyote. I can still sit down and watch TV and suddenly I am in it! *(laughs, takes paperback book from back pocket)* It is why I now prefer a good book.

TAGGART. It was like no dream I ever had before…or did I?

PEPITO. It's all right, David. Rest.

TAGGART. I was married. A nice girl, a real nice girl. We had a couple of kids – daughters. In my dream one of them screamed.

TWO CHILDREN'S VOICES. Ring around the rosy! Pocketful of posy! Ashes, ashes! We all fall down!

PEPITO. *(grins as he and **TAGGART** look off toward **VOICES**)* Of course. You heard the child.

TAGGART. Yes! But…it was so real. You don't know. My wife and I…made love. It was beautiful.

PEPITO. *(sighs)* Always in a dream it is beautiful.

TAGGART. *(a sudden, fearful realization)* We're at my…sister's?

PEPITO. I called her at the store. She'll be here quickly.

TAGGART. *(anxiety growing)* Not my sister's!

PEPITO. I told you, we needed a place to hide from Sligo. What is wrong, my friend?

TAGGART. But not my *sister's!*

> (**MEREDITH**, *a pinched-looking, hard-working woman in a cheap cloth coat – played by the same actress who plays **FRAN** – enters.*)

MEREDITH. David, are you here?

TAGGART. *(barely audible, as he turns from her)* Not my sister's…

MEREDITH. *(momentarily blocked by **PEPITO**)* Pepito! Where is – *(sees him)* David! What have they done to you?

TAGGART. *(determinedly facing away)* Don't, Meredith. I don't want to see you.

MEREDITH. *(does not understand)* David?

PEPITO. *(intercedes, tries to explain)* They hurt him. They hit his head.

MEREDITH. *(rushes to* **TAGGART***, holds him)* Oh! My! David! *(rocks him, soothing)* I warned you, don't you remember? Stay away from those big boys. *(as* **PEPITO** *regards her curiously)* Oh, this has all happened before! He was only a child! I told him, those boys are too big for you. But would he listen? No! A boy took a stick —

TAGGART. *(Disgusted; he's said this a hundred times before.)* It slipped.

MEREDITH. That's what *he* told *you! (to* **PEPITO***)* It was terrible! He came in *hurt,* the blood just pouring from above his eye! And it was me who had to take care of him, who had to tell those rowdies, "You get out of here! Get right down those stairs!" I threw the rollerskates at them.

TAGGART. *(who'd forgotten this part)* Rollerskates?

(A shadowy **FIGURE** *— perhaps a boy, perhaps not — appears just outside the circle of light.* **MEREDITH** *stares at him angrily, challenging.)*

MEREDITH. I hit one. He swore at me. I still remember the filth of his mouth.

THE FIGURE. You didn't even hurt me! *(Bronx cheer:)* Ppmmft!

*(***THE FIGURE*** *retreats back into the shadows.)*

TAGGART. That boy was trying to help!

MEREDITH. *(to* **PEPITO***)* David always said that. He was so forgiving.

PEPITO. *(can't resist it)* You were a good boy, David. *(laughs, pretending to retreat as* **MEREDITH** *stares at him angrily)*

MEREDITH. *(attention back on* **TAGGART***)* That settles it. You won't go back to that terrible Halfway House. You'll stay with me, the way you were supposed to, the way Mommy wanted. Everything will be like it was…before.

TAGGART. *(a protest weakened by his physical condition)* Meredith, I…

MEREDITH. *(impulsively embraces him)* David-love…David!

TAGGART. DON'T! *(pushes her away, finds the will to get to his feet)* I can't…stay. Pepito?

PEPITO. *(braces him reluctantly)* I see danger out there.

TAGGART. Just out there? Not *here?*

> *(He would leave, but his whole world begins to spin; he grabs his head, sinks toward the bed.)*

Ohhh...

MEREDITH. *(lights beginning to fall)* David? What changed? Why can't we...Why can't we live together like before?

> *(Lights are down in* **MEREDITH***'s room, her last words lingering in the blackness. Lights then slowly rise in* **ROSS***'s office.* **ROSS** *sits at his desk, asleep.* **CHARLIE BISHOP***, a casual, brisk and highly intelligent African-American, enters, touches* **ROSS***'s shoulder.)*

CHARLIE. Dave!...Yo, Dave.

ROSS. *(awakens with a start, looks around)* What?

CHARLIE. *(backs off, lightly)* Ha! You don't come up swinging. It's good to know. *(as* **ROSS** *continues to look around, disoriented)* What's the matter? Not getting enough at home? Sleep, I mean.

ROSS. *(as it comes back to him, embarrassed)* Forgive me, Charlie. Must have dozed off. I was reading... *(finds it in front of him)* your brief.

CHARLIE. *(looks at brief, makes a face)* Stinks, right? I get the bastards off. *(when* **ROSS** *does not respond:)* You awake?

ROSS. *(momentarily uncertain)* Yeah, sure. *(clicks intercom)* Becky.

BECKY'S VOICE. *(over intercom)* Yes sir.

ROSS. Get some coffee in here.

BECKY'S VOICE. *(over intercom, somehow too eager)* Yes sir!

ROSS. *(looks at brief again.)* So you get them off. What about it?

CHARLIE. Well, hell, I feel like window dressing, just bringing it up. And they swore they hired me for my brain, Dave, not my dynamic black profile.

ROSS. *(skim-reading brief, turns a page)* Get to the point, counselor.

CHARLIE. I don't know about you, but I consider myself a young idealist. I've even thought about having those two words, "Young Idealist," stamped on my shorts. Beats the hell out of "Fruit of the Loom," right?

ROSS. *(rueful, patient)* Charlie...get to the point.

CHARLIE. I am! The fact is – *(and now the seriousness, near-bitterness come out:)* I hate like hell defending drug pushers.

ROSS. Drug pushers? What are you saying? We're a corporate law office.

CHARLIE. Pepper Pharmaceuticals is a corporate drug pusher. So say the FDA. And I think they're right for a change.

ROSS. *(looks hard at the brief, his dream returning)* Drug pushers...drug users.

PEPITO'S VOICE. Ex-drug users.

ROSS. *(who has heard the voice only internally)* Ex-drug users. *(looks sharply at* **CHARLIE**, *the dream gone)* It just occurred to me. I was dreaming about drugs. *(feels better as he realizes:)* Your brief! *That's* where I got it.

CHARLIE. *(interested, understanding)* Sounds wild.

ROSS. *(laughs softly, in a much better mood)* It gets wilder. I also dreamed – *(His laughter stops, the memory too vivid.)* Oh hell.

CHARLIE. *(prompting, curious)* Yeah?

ROSS. Well... *(On the spot, feels he has to continue, laughs again, but the laugh is obviously forced.)* I dreamed my wife was really my sister.

CHARLIE. *(considers this)* Your wife – your sister? *(a subtle grin)* Where I come from, they got a word for people like you. In fact, they got a couple of words.

ROSS. *(a careful admonition)* Charlie...

*(**BECKY**, attractive in her early twenties, enters with a large Styrofoam coffee cup.)*

BECKY. *(so brightly you might think she has a crush on him)* Mr. Ross, I have your – Ow! Spilled it.

(Transfers cup to other hand, sets cup on desk as she sucks at and shakes her scalded fingers; reaches for what might be an important piece of paper on **ROSS***'s desk – a possible impending tragedy which* **ROSS** *warns her against by immediately withdrawing the paper; as she backs off in apology and confusion:)*

I'll get something…wipe it up. *(stops before exiting)* Can I bring you some coffee, Mr. Bishop?

CHARLIE. *(smiles tightly)* I'll spare you the pain.

*(***BECKY*** *giggles and exits quickly.)*

(looking after her, muses) How long has Becky been with us?

ROSS. I don't know – seven months.

CHARLIE. *(sighs)* Why do I always think it's her first day?

ROSS. *(ignores the comment, concentrates on the brief)* Strange… your arguments seem familiar.

CHARLIE. *(his attention snapping back)* Huh? They *should*, don't you think? I mean, I obviously based them on *your* arguments.

ROSS. *(not understanding)* Mine?

CHARLIE. Sure. When *you* got Pepper off. *(as* **ROSS** *shakes his head, trying to remember)* Come on, Dave. I know you've handled a lot of cases since, but you couldn't have forgotten *that* one. You showed the government had no prima facie evidence. They couldn't even bring it to trial.

ROSS. *(although he still does not recall with any degree of certainty)* Oh…yeah.

CHARLIE. *(sees something is disturbing him)* David…are you all right?

PEPITO'S VOICE. They hurt him. They hit his head.

ROSS. *(snaps to; again the dream is gone)* I'm fine…OK, *I* got them off, now *you* get them off. What about it?

CHARLIE. Don't you read me, Dave? I don't *want* to get them off. There was a rumor, two years ago, about suppressed evidence…

ROSS. *(too quickly)* I don't know what you're talking about.

CHARLIE. Papers of incorporation proving officers at Pepper own the dummy companies they ship the junk to below the border. You heard the rumor…

ROSS. *(again too quickly)* No.

CHARLIE. *(finds this hard to believe)* Well, everybody else did. See, I thought if I could get my hands on those papers…

ROSS. *(stares hard at him)* You'd do what?

CHARLIE. Well, I'd…I don't know. *(then:)* I'd put them in a plain brown envelope and send them to Jack Miles.

ROSS. *(amazement)* Pepper is your *client!*

CHARLIE. Pepper is guilty!

ROSS. But they're *not* guilty! Not till a judge *says* they're guilty.

CHARLIE. *(topping him)* They're *morally* guilty! Or doesn't that count anymore?

ROSS. Damn it, Charlie – who are you to judge? Your sworn duty is to defend Pepper, guilty or not – and you've just got to learn to live with it.

CHARLIE. *(thinks hard about this)* To live with what? Their guilt? Or mine?

(Before **ROSS** *can reply,* **BECKY** *enters with some paper towels, begins to wipe up spill.)*

(grins, relaxing) Anyhow, I don't have the evidence. So…the hell with it.

(Starts out but momentarily pauses behind **BECKY***, who is now on all fours. Clearly he is tempted to take a swat at her backside, but then:)*

Discipline, Charles. Discipline.

(**CHARLIE** *quickly exits as* **BECKY** *straightens, looks from* **ROSS** *to where* **CHARLIE** *exited and back again, not at all sure what* **CHARLIE** *meant.* **ROSS** *meanwhile has discovered a stack of call slips, wet from the spilled coffee, on his desk.*)

ROSS. Becky, *what* are these?

BECKY. *(no idea)* Those? *(gets very close to him in order to see)* Oh, those are phone calls.

ROSS. *(more a statement than a question)* For me?

BECKY. *(who can't understand why he is quietly angry)* Yes sir.

ROSS. *(a sudden but tempered explosion)* They all came in this morning!

BECKY. *(intimidated) Yes* sir.

ROSS. *(overly patient, tries to explain)* How is it I didn't receive any of these calls?

BECKY. *(finally understands his concern)* Oh! Well, the thing is, what I mean – I mean, Mr. Ross, well – I kept looking in your office, and you were – what I mean to say, sir, you were — Well, you know what your were.

ROSS. *(supplies the missing word)* Asleep.

BECKY. *(a very small voice)* Yes sir.

ROSS. *(grins ruefully; there is no way he can stay mad at her)* In the future, if I am asleep at my desk, will you kindly waken me?

BECKY. Certainly, sir!

ROSS. And Becky, will you forget this "sir" stuff? I think you know me well enough to start calling me David.

BECKY. Whatever you say, sir – David. Oh! That doesn't sound right. I'd better practice it.

ROSS. *(frankly enjoying her)* You'd better.

BECKY. Yes... *(starts to leave but stops suddenly)* David?

ROSS. *(who had returned to his work, looks up)* Hmmm?

BECKY. *(all in a rush)* Do you think I know you well enough to come to your anniversary party?

ROSS. *(doesn't understand this at all)* Well, I don't – uh...

BECKY. That didn't sound right either. What I mean is, I've been invited – by Jack Miles.

ROSS. *(surprise)* You know Jack Miles?

BECKY. Well, that's the thing of it – I don't. *(as he waits for further explanation)* What happened, Mr. Miles – oh, he wants me to call him Jack –

ROSS. I guess he *would*.

BECKY. His note's in there. He called this morning while you were…

ROSS. *(delicately)* Asleep.

BECKY. Yes sir. He said he wanted to RSVP your invitation and – we got to talking. *(corrects herself)* He got to talking. He was very nice…persuasive.

ROSS. Jack Miles is both of those.

BECKY. Anyhow, he asked me to be his date. I said I couldn't…then I said I could – but just to get rid of him, you know? – only, I mean, I don't *want* to get rid of him. I want to *go*. But then again, I *don't* want to go. *(miserable)* I mean, I'm sure I did the wrong thing in there somewhere.

ROSS. *(supremely tolerant)* I'm not so sure. Jack Miles is what the society columnists are prone to call a "most eligible bachelor." I don't think you'll be disappointed.

BECKY. *(happy)* You mean it's all right if I go?

ROSS. *(thought he'd made it clear)* Yes!

BECKY. *(a sudden thought)* You don't think *he'll* be disappointed?

ROSS. *(distracted, looks up)* What?

BECKY. I withdraw the question.

ROSS. Will *Jack* be disappointed? Let me put it succinctly: No.

BECKY. *(starts to back out, uncertain)* That's kind of you to say…

ROSS. It's true. Jack and I both used to date Fran. So I guess you'd say our tastes in women run pretty close. And if I were ten percent less married than I am…

BECKY. Sir?

ROSS. I'd probably be chasing you around this desk right now.

BECKY. *(backs abruptly)* Sir!

ROSS. *(intentionally gruff)* Get out of here. Go to lunch. Let me do my work.

BECKY. *(relief)* Yes sir! Thank you, sir!

(**BECKY** *exits.*)

ROSS. *(calls after her)* And call me David! *(laughs)* Chasing her around the desk...how'd I come up with *that*? *(looks at brief and then away, muses)* Chasing her around the desk... *(stares into space, his face changing subtly as he sips his coffee)* Chasing her...

(Lights remain up in Office as they rise in Bar. **TAGGART** *sits in exactly the same position as* **ROSS***, sipping from an almost empty stein of beer and staring directly at* **ROSS***.* **PEPITO***, also with a beer, sits beside him, reading a paperback.)*

ANNOUNCER'S VOICE. Join us tomorrow when Miles Detergents presents the next episode of our continuing story.

PEPITO. *(looks up sharply, follows* **TAGGART** *'s stare)* How can you watch such garbage? *(calls out)* Julio! Por favor! Shut the damn thing off!

(Lights drop immediately in Office; **TAGGART** *turns to* **PEPITO** *in anger.)*

TAGGART. What'd you do *that* for?

PEPITO. *(a soft answer)* I am surprised, David, to find you an aficionado of the soap opera. Such troubled lives – oh, madre! The boy has a lovely querida at home but is heartbroken because he can't have one at the office too! *(laughs)*

TAGGART. Is *that* what it was, television?

PEPITO. *(studies him)* You don't remember?

TAGGART. *(as he realizes)* I was *in* it. I was one of the actors.

PEPITO. So it has happened! Well, do not panic, David. It may only be the blow to your head. Barely three weeks have passed. In time you will overcome it.

TAGGART. Three weeks? I remember only one day. We were at my sister's.

PEPITO. You insisted we leave. Why I still don't know. We have since been at the Halfway House. It was your argument Sligo would not dare encounter you before witnesses. So far, events have proved you right, but – *(apprehensive)* I do not like coming here – to the cantina. Cantinas have a way of becoming very empty very quickly.

TAGGART. *(at last, a confession)* Pepito…I was in my other world again.

PEPITO. Your dream?

TAGGART. That's what I meant: my dream.

PEPITO. *(warm)* With the beautiful wife and niñas.

TAGGART. *(reconstructing)* But they weren't there. I was in an office. *(remembers)* A lawyer! I was a lawyer.

PEPITO. You are intelligent. If you were not so honest, you *could* be a lawyer.

TAGGART. But I don't know anything about it! I was reading a…brief. That's what I called it. About drugs.

PEPITO. *That* you know about.

TAGGART. This black guy I was talking to, I tried to tell him about *us* – and I laughed! That's how sure I was what's happening here is only…that I myself am only…a dream, a fantasy in someone else's imagination.

PEPITO. *(concern)* My friend, do not excite yourself.

TAGGART. When I was a kid, I – I thought about being a lawyer…good hours, you own your own home – wife, couple of kids, people calling you "Counselor"…it'd be nice.

PEPITO. At a distance, many things are nice.

TAGGART. *(strangely)* But…am I *at* a distance?

PEPITO. What? Oh, I comprehend. Yes! You look at me, Pepito, and you think, "Maybe the Chicano is part of my dream!" Amigo, tu esta vulvindo loco.

TAGGART. What?

PEPITO. You speak no Spanish, do you, David?

TAGGART. No…

PEPITO. Yet you have just heard me speak it. Now how can you hear me say distinctly a language you do not understand?

TAGGART. You could be saying anything.

PEPITO. But I did not say "anything." I said: *(slowly)* Amigo, tu esta vulvindo loco. You can say it too. Say it!

TAGGART. Amigo, tu esta…

PEPITO. Vulvindo loco.

TAGGART. Amigo, tu esta vulvindo loco.

PEPITO. Perfect!

TAGGART. What does it mean?

PEPITO. Mean? *(laughs)* It means, "My friend, you are going crazy." *(laughs again)*

TAGGART. Not very funny.

PEPITO. Forgive me. I tease you, David. I joke. I try to help you rise from your mood. Here is a much simpler test. Feel your hands. *(**TAGGART** does.)* Now your face…your nose…your chin…Could you do that in a dream?

TAGGART. I don't…know.

PEPITO. *(chides him)* Then I will tell you. You could *not* do that in a dream! Take my word for it, David. Trust me.

TAGGART. I trust…my own senses, Pepito. I know. I *know.* It's all right.

*(**ANITA** enters. She is the same actress who played **BECKY** but now wears a waitress outfit which does nothing to hide her ample figure. She projects an earth-mother familiarity with the men.)*

ANITA. How about it, fellas? Another round?

TAGGART. *(surprise)* Becky?

ANITA. Try Anita.

TAGGART. *(confused, trying to accept the name)* Anita…?

(She takes his stein and reaches for **PEPITO***'s.)*

PEPITO. *(refuses to yield it)* Thank you, not at this time.

ANITA. Whatever you say.

(A final smile at **TAGGART** *before she exits, her hips swinging lazily with her walk.* **TAGGART** *stares after her, transfixed.)*

PEPITO. *(follows* **TAGGART***'s gaze)* Charming…yes. Ah, were *I* to fantasize, I would fantasize about *her.*

TAGGART. I…*have.*

PEPITO. *(interested)* She was in your dream?

TAGGART. …Yes.

PEPITO. And you and she, you…?

TAGGART. *(shakes his head)* No.

PEPITO. *(sighs)* A wasted opportunity. It is my understanding Anita plays – but for pay, good pay. She belongs to the management here. They esteem her services highly.

TAGGART. *(A spark has been struck.)* The management?

PEPITO. Blackman. You know the hombre – the black man who calls himself Blackman. He is another reason I did not wish to come here.

TAGGART. Blackman? *(relief)* Pepito, I just remembered why we *did.*

*(***ANITA** *enters with a stein of beer for* **TAGGART***.)*

ANITA. *(knowingly)* Will there be…anything else?

TAGGART. *(sudden authority)* Tell Blackman I want him.

PEPITO. *(surprise)* David!

ANITA. *(smartly)* Can I tell him who you are?

TAGGART. David Taggart.

ANITA. Can I tell him who *that* is?

TAGGART. A man…who may have a parcel.

ANITA. Oh? *(takes a step back, looks from* TAGGART *to* PEPITO *and back, frightened, eager, trying not to show it.)* I'll see if he's...busy.

(exits quickly)

PEPITO. *(starts to rise)* I am leaving, David.

TAGGART. *(takes his arm)* Stay, Pepito. I need you.

PEPITO. *(cold, bitter)* You are twice a fool. Once to take the parcel – again to think you can deal with Blackman. *(pulls away)* We have scheduled an encounter at the House tonight. Will you be there to help your friends stop using drugs?

TAGGART. But we've never used drugs – they've used us! Once...let's turn it around. The parcel's got to be worth a fortune.

*(*PEPITO *starts away.)*

You don't *understand!* It can mean a fresh start for both of us!

PEPITO. *(simply, with dignity)* You, David, do not understand. I *have* my fresh start.

(begins to exit, but turns suddenly, bitingly)

And you *could* be a lawyer.

(exits)

*(*BLACKMAN *enters behind* TAGGART. *He is the same actor who played* CHARLIE, *but seems larger, stronger. He wears a dashiki, shades, and an aura of evil tempered by an immense tolerance for other men's weaknesses. As* TAGGART *turns,* BLACKMAN *is already sitting, facing him.)*

BLACKMAN. You wanted to see me, Charlie?

TAGGART. I'm Taggart – David Taggart.

BLACKMAN. You don't mind if I call you Charlie, do you? You call me Blackman. It'll keep us straight.

TAGGART. The waitress, Anita, told you what I...might have?

BLACKMAN. She said you found a parcel. As chief honcho, lost and found falls within my domain. Can you describe the parcel?

TAGGART. Isn't it up to the loser to describe it?

BLACKMAN. *(shrugs)* Man, I never said I lost it. *(takes off his glasses, the better to see **TAGGART**)* You looking at me funny. I remind you of someone?

TAGGART. *(as he perceives the resemblance)* Geez, you *do*.

BLACKMAN. *(an easy shrug)* But then...all us black mothers look alike. *(puts the glasses back on)* What were we discussing?

TAGGART. *(carefully)* I understand there's a reward...for the parcel.

BLACKMAN. You really want me to offer a reward for something I maybe never lost?

TAGGART. Why not?

BLACKMAN. *(after a pause)* You know, Charlie, I don't like you. I don't like you because you're dumb. You're dumb because you talk in circles with me – *me* who has little time to waste these days. I told you I want to know about the parcel, and I hope you take me at face value when I say there are other people right here in this establishment who also want to know. *(with a smile)* Some not nearly so polite as me. So do you talk to me...or them?

TAGGART. *(temper rising)* Sligo tried to beat it out of me. He couldn't, you won't – they won't either.

BLACKMAN. *(relaxes for the first time)* Oh, that was *you!* *(laughs)* Hey, baby, I dig! I make you! *(picks up stein)* What you got here – brew? Man, you insult my hospitality! *(calls out)* My girl! A little sipping Scotch here!

ANITA. *(off)* Yes sir!

BLACKMAN. *(chuckles)* Cute, ain't it? She always calls me sir. You know, you and me, we got a fierce common bond. Deep in our guts, Charlie, we hate the same pig – Lieutenant Detective Sligo. *(spits)* Goddam honky's operating in the same business as you and me!

(ANITA enters with two Scotches.)

BLACKMAN. *(cont.)* No bottle? Come on, girl. Have you forgot how we treat distinguished guests?

ANITA. *(nervous around* **BLACKMAN** *– for she is deathly afraid of him)* I'm sorry. I'll get it.

(She exits, **TAGGART** *again looking after her and* **BLACKMAN** *observing him.)*

BLACKMAN. *(perceptive)* You like that? I can fix it. Tell me what you want, white brother. Anything. See if I can't fix it.

TAGGART. What I want, Blackman, is…

(He freezes as **ANITA** *returns with bottle, sets it down between the men, looks nervously from one to the other, and exits.)*

TAGGART. Fifty thousand dollars.

BLACKMAN. *(softly)* Ooo-eee! You *are* looking for a reward! *(knocks back the Scotch, pours another, then:)* I only paid that much for the original purchase.

TAGGART. Don't put me on, Blackman. I know the price of eggs. That purchase had to cost at least two hundred K.

BLACKMAN. But fifty *more?* I was thinking…maybe twenty-five.

TAGGART. Keep thinking.

BLACKMAN. You got something you're planning to do with all that bread?

TAGGART. I got ways to use it, yeah.

BLACKMAN. To use it? Yeah…*(considers this a moment, studying* **TAGGART***)* You know, white brother, maybe you and I *can* work something out. Suppose I lay on twenty-five for the parcel…

TAGGART. I told you fifty.

BLACKMAN. Hear me out, Charlie. Twenty-five for the parcel – the same again for Sligo.

TAGGART. Sligo?

BLACKMAN. *(shrugs)* He's favorite people to neither you nor me. You get what you want, I get what I want, we get what we want.

TAGGART. *(considers this)* I don't know.

BLACKMAN. *(a taunt)* Course, maybe you never wasted nobody…

TAGGART. I was Special Forces in Kabul. It's where I picked up the habit.

BLACKMAN. *Which* habit?

TAGGART. I don't know. *(takes a beat before:)* Maybe both.

BLACKMAN. You're thinking, my way, friend. *(a sudden laugh)* Keep thinking! The world won't boil over before noon tomorrow. In the meanswhile…

(Snaps his fingers, ANITA appears.)

Little mother, this white john wants to get into your pants.

ANITA. *(stares frankly at TAGGART)* Do you?

TAGGART. *(angry, uncomfortable)* You got a hell of a way of putting things, Blackman.

ANITA. *(much closer to TAGGART, seductive)* Do you?

TAGGART. I've been waiting…seven months.

ANITA. Oh! *(She has upset TAGGART's glass.)* I'll get something – wipe it up.

TAGGART. Leave it!

BLACKMAN. *(who is fully in command here)* It's cool, honey-roll.

(as TAGGART begins to lead her off:)

Take the rest of the night off, why don't you? Make it worth his while.

(With the two having exited, calls off.)

Julio! We got anything to eat? Stuffed olives? Anything? I'm hungry!

(The lights start down and we hear:)

FRAN'S VOICE. How long does it take to get stuffed olives?

(Blackout in bar, lights up full in kitchen. **DAVID ROSS** *stands at the table, an olive bottle in his hand.* **FRAN** *stands at his side.)*

ROSS. *(suddenly aware, opens bottle)* I'm sorry, Fran. Daydreaming. *(begins to put the olives in a small glass bowl)*

FRAN. *(concern for him)* You've been out here half an hour, honey. Your guests are wondering about you.

ROSS. *(concentrates on his work)* Let them. *(suddenly faces her)* What the hell...I was in the dream again.

FRAN. *(greater concern)* Just now?

ROSS. *(nods with vehemence)* Damn! I'm starting to have it as a...*daydream.* I came out here to get the olives and suddenly I was *there.* It was so real. So...real.

*(***CHARLIE BISHOP** *steps into the light frame, dressed for the party.)*

CHARLIE. Hey, you two going to join your own party?

FRAN. We'll be right there, Charlie.

CHARLIE. *(picks the bowl of olives up)* Excuse me. Dying for some olives.

(Pops one in his mouth as he exits with the bowl, **ROSS** *staring after him.)*

FRAN. David, will you do me a favor? Please? Will you talk to Jack Miles?

ROSS. *(surprised)* Jack? He's a U.S. Attorney. What does *he* know about – whatever the hell it is that's bothering me?

FRAN. He's your friend, David.

ROSS. Whose friend?

FRAN. All right – our friend.

ROSS. *(after a moment)* I'll talk to him.

FRAN. When?

ROSS. Soon.

FRAN. Tonight?

ROSS. All right, tonight.

(JACK MILES *and* BECKY *erupt into the scene,* JACK*'s arm about* BECKY*'s waist.* JACK *is played by the same actor who plays* PEPITO *but seems entirely different in this role. There is no trace of an accent and lifts or fashionable heels add to his height.*)

JACK. *(more convivial than intoxicated)* So this is where the lovebirds have flown! *Thought* we might catch you in a corner someplace.

ROSS. *(perfectly sober)* Hello, Jack…Becky.

JACK. Wonderful girl you've got here, Dave. She just made me a perfectly immodest proposal.

BECKY. *(who of course did not)* Mr. Miles!

JACK. *(holds her tighter)* Jack, honey, Jack. *(to* ROSS*)* No wonder you never introduced us. With one like this at the office and one like this at home – *(His other arm goes around* FRAN*'s waist.)* why spoil things, huh?

FRAN. *(pulls away sharply)* Please, Jack!

JACK. *(releases* BECKY *also as he sees something is wrong)* Not funny, ha?

FRAN. *(controlled anger)* Not very. No.

BECKY. *(embarrassed, straightens her dress)* If you all will excuse me…

(laughs nervously and exits)

JACK. *(contrite)* Say, I'm sorry. *(looks from* FRAN *to* ROSS*, trying to read their expressions)* What is it? Someone sick? One of the kids?

FRAN. Nothing like that, no.

JACK. What *is* it?

FRAN. David…?

ROSS. All right.

*(FRAN *exits* JACK *looks after her and back to* ROSS*.)*

JACK. Well, go ahead, Davey. What –

ROSS. *(interrupts flatly)* Jack, do you speak any Spanish?

JACK. *(surprised at the question)* Spanish?

ROSS. *(insists)* Do you?

JACK. No.

ROSS. Too bad. I just this minute realized you're the spitting image of another dear friend. His name is Pepito, he comes from Mexico – I think. And he speaks Spanish fluently.

*(**JACK** listens as the lights in the kitchen dim to black. They rise immediately – but dimly – in **ANITA**'s bedroom. She is alone and seemingly nude except for the silk robe she is tying loosely about her. **TAGGART** enters the light frame, turns her around to face him, and slips his arms inside the robe and about her body.)*

ANITA. *(laughs, kisses him)* It'll be fun, Davey. I promise you. More fun than you ever dreamed.

*(Lights dim to black in the bedroom and come up full in the kitchen once more. **ROSS** and **JACK** have changed positions. **JACK**, his suitcoat off, sits against the edge of the table, listening.)*

ROSS. *(pacing)* And even as I spoke to you just now, I was – for a minute – back there. The girl – the prostitute – and I were in her bedroom. We were doing…what two people do in a bedroom.

JACK. Just *now* this happened?

ROSS. Yes.

JACK. You enjoyed it?

ROSS. *(in tortured candor)* What's tearing at my guts is…I'm enjoying the whole damn thing! In some ways…it beats the hell out of suburbia.

JACK. In this dream – hallucination – whatever it is – you say I am Pepito.

ROSS. You sure as hell are.

JACK. Any others there you know?

ROSS. Maybe.

JACK. You'd rather not say? *(when* **ROSS** *makes no reply:)* You'd rather not say. *(after a moment:)* What kind of drugs are you into?

ROSS. Drugs? Seconal when I need it...to go to sleep.

JACK. That's it?

ROSS. Valium. Not every day though. Just when I'm...really tense. I've got a doctor's prescription.

JACK. Anything else?

ROSS. Yes, damn it! Tylenol!

JACK. Easy. I'm just asking.

ROSS. Hell...

(walks away, disgusted)

JACK. Something else I've got to ask...As I talk to you now, are you entirely convinced this is the reality – the other is the dream?

ROSS. Why should you ask that?

JACK. No evasions, Dave. Are you convinced?

ROSS. *(quietly)* Yes.

JACK. I didn't hear you.

ROSS. *Yes! Yes! I'm convinced! (a beat, and then quietly:)* The only problem is...In the dream I'm *also* convinced. You don't know, Jack. It seems to have a logic of its own. In the bar I had practically the same conversation with Pepito I'm having with *you!* He gave me a test...

(During this last **JACK** *has pensively strode upstage past the edge of the circle of light, his back to* **ROSS**. *In the shadows, he turns, and is briefly* **PEPITO**.)

PEPITO. Feel your hands...feel your face...*(turns away again)*

ROSS. *(feels hands and face as he speaks)* I *felt* them. They there were *there. I* was there.

JACK. *(returns to* **ROSS***)* You don't need any advice from me, Davey. You *know* what your next move is.

ROSS. ...Do I?

JACK. The same move you'd want me to make if I were going through what you are.

ROSS. See a doctor, you mean. A psychiatrist.

JACK. Is it so hard to say? It's only logical.

ROSS. I'm learning to distrust logic.

JACK. You know, there may be nothing at all wrong with your mind…It could be something physical. A lesion, a benign tumor.

ROSS. *(sighs)* Beautiful word, "benign."

JACK. What I'm saying is, a psychiatrist is also an M.D. He'll give you all the tests. The more possibilities we can eliminate, the closer we are to an answer. You know you have to do this.

ROSS. *(after a moment, the last words hanging in the air)* Yes.

(**FRAN** *enters.*)

FRAN. How's it going?

JACK. Very well, as a matter of fact.

ROSS. *(turns away)* Super.

JACK. Davey – fill her in, ha?

*(With **ROSS** still turned away, she raises her hands in silent questions to* **JACK**. **JACK** *returns the gesture and exits.)*

ROSS. *(after a moment)* I've decided…I'm going to see a shrink.

FRAN. *(careful not to show her relief)* I suppose it's the best thing.

ROSS. It's the only thing.

FRAN. *(close to him)* I saved a little Pink Chablis. When everybody goes, we'll have a quiet drink together.

ROSS. In prelude?

FRAN. *(softly)* Honey, it's almost a month now.

ROSS. *(sardonic)* Not that we haven't tried.

FRAN. I know, David. *(brushes his cheek with her lips)* Tonight we'll try again…okay?

ROSS. *(who would please her)* Sure, we'll try again.

> *(FRAN exits. When she is gone, ROSS touches his cheek where she kissed him. Then, unable to stop himself, he touches his nose and chin as before. After a moment, quietly:)*

ROSS. Amigo, tu esta vulvindo loco.

> *(Lights fall to black and rise in ANITA's bedroom. TAGGART, wearing only underwear and alone in bed, sits up.)*

TAGGART. *(looks around, just waking)* Anita…? Anita! What? *(finds a note pinned to the pillow, chuckles)* I thought the man was supposed to leave the note. *(opens it, reads)* "Darling David." Hmmm. "Couldn't bear to wake you. Ran out for a minute to buy us breakfast. Thanks for everything." *(grins)* "Everything" underlined three times. "P.S. Do you know you talk in your sleep? Who's Jack? Who's Fran? If that's a girl, I'm jealous." *(frowns, having forgotten the dream)* Talk in my…? Oh. Jack Miles – Pepito without the accent. *(shakes his head, not upset)* Crazy dreams.

> *(He has begun to dress – his pants and then his shirt. There are footsteps off. He calls.)*

Come in, Anita! You've got the key!

SLIGO'S VOICE. Ah, lad, Anita I'm not.

TAGGART. Sligo!

> *(SLIGO enters the light frame. We see him clearly for the first time. He is a large, powerful man, running heavily to fat. He smiles often, but his smile is crueler than his frown.)*

SLIGO. We waited till the darling little girl went down to the market. A couple of my boys are detaining her – not for long, mind you – but long enough. I've come to talk to you about a parcel, Davey. Do you know where I might be able to lay my hands on one?

TAGGART. Look, if you've got a warrant –

SLIGO. Warrants, lad, are for inexperienced officers, good, young men who wish to try their cases in court. But as one matures in the police department – a rapid process, I don't mind saying – one learns some cases are better settled *out* of court. Yours is such a case, Davey-boy. You and I can settle it right here in this room. No one will be the wiser.

TAGGART. Listen, Sligo –

SLIGO. Lad, I've only one question: Where is the parcel?

TAGGART. I don't know what you're –

SLIGO. *(interrupts)* You were observed sipping Scotch with a certain Mr. Blackman. Mr. Blackman is quite the snob, you know, most particular about his Scotch-sipping companions. It seems an arrangement is being made. I'd very much appreciate whatever details you may be willing to offer.

(He has taken a small pistol out of his pocket.)

TAGGART. *(uncertainly)* You intend to *shoot* me?

SLIGO. *(laughs)* With this, lad? Why, it's not much more than a cap pistol! In the department we call them Saturday night specials. Sometimes we call them drop guns.

(He drops it on the bed. **TAGGART** *takes a step toward it but* **SLIGO** *smoothly produces another pistol, a much larger and quite menacing .38.)*

That's right. Reach for it.

*(***TAGGART*** *freezes.)*

Wise lad. *(beat)* In a moment I'll begin some target practice. The idea is to put the bullet where it can most hurt but do the least permanent damage – except perhaps to your relationship with young Anita. When I do that, you'll reach for the drop gun – or you won't. In which case, I'll put another bullet in you. Then perhaps you'll reach for it. But if you remain stubborn…Well, this game can continue a long while. Extremely long, for you. In any case, my final bullet will be through your head, and when I phone my captain, the drop gun – I guarantee – will be in your hand.

(He waits but **TAGGART** *says nothing.)*

SLIGO. *(cont.)* I suppose I should caution you: Once begun, this game is most difficult to stop.

(as **TAGGART***, quietly terrified, inadvertently shifts his weight:)*

Ah, don't turn away, lad. I want my first shot to be a clean one.

TAGGART. *(the words coming out by themselves)* I don't have the parcel with me.

SLIGO. *(smiles, relaxing)* I never thought you did.

TAGGART. I can get it.

SLIGO. When?

TAGGART. Tomorrow.

SLIGO. Too long.

TAGGART. Tonight.

SLIGO. Better.

TAGGART. I'll bring it to you.

SLIGO. Where?

TAGGART. ...The station?

SLIGO. *(laughs)* Lord no, not the station.

TAGGART. You tell me.

SLIGO. Some neutral ground, I think. Second Avenue, near the Halfway House.

TAGGART. Second and Grand.

SLIGO. Second and Grand it is, lad. Ten o'clock.

(returns both guns to his person)

And now, so you'll be sure to be on time...

(Taking **TAGGART***'s shoulders, he turns him so that his back is to the audience. Blocked by* **TAGGART***, we do not see what* **SLIGO** *does, but* **TAGGART** *is suddenly doubled up in pain.)*

SLIGO. *(easy, as always)* Next time, you know, I'll not explain the rules. I'll merely start the game.

(SLIGO exits.)

TAGGART. *(falls on the bed, knees locked together in pain)* Oh, God.

(ANITA dashes in, frantic.)

ANITA. Davey!

TAGGART. *(cannot bear to be touched)* Stay away!

ANITA. *(starts off)* I've got some junk. I'll get it.

TAGGART. *(a scream)* No!...No junk. Call...Blackman. Tell him it's on. Fifty K. Got that? Fifty K!

(TAGGART's head falls forward. The lights go to black in the bedroom and rise in the psychiatrist's office. ROSS sits on a straight chair before the desk. The psychiatrist, DR. PEMBERTON, sits with his back to us.)

ROSS. ...And that's where it stopped.

PEPITO. You left it right there?

ROSS. That's where it ended, yes.

(PEMBERTON turns in his chair. We see it is the same actor who played SLIGO. But he has no brogue, wears glasses and certainly seems to be an entirely kind and good man. And he is holding a half-sandwich.)

PEMBERTON. And you say this Sligo look like me?

ROSS. Strangely enough, he *does*. I don't know what significance is.

PEMBERTON. *(takes a bite of the sandwich)* Mmmm.

ROSS. Did you say something, doctor?

PEMBERTON. No, just taking a bite of my sandwich. *(takes another bite, chews thoughtfully)* Whom did you meet first, David – Sligo or me?

ROSS. This is what, my sixth, seventh visit?

PEMBERTON. Whichever.

ROSS. I was about to say Sligo. But now, thinking about it, I never actually *saw* him that first time. I just heard his voice. That soft Irish brogue. There were lights in my eyes.

PEMBERTON. *(checks a scribbled notepad)* Oh yes. *(Then uses a finger to wipe away a crumb or dollop of mustard from the notepad, sucking the finger after doing so.)*

ROSS. So I knew you first, Dr. Pemberton. There's no Irish in you, is there?

PEMBERTON. If there is, my mother isn't saying. Curious, the name Sligo. It's not a common name.

ROSS. I checked a couple of big city directories. I couldn't find it.

PEMBERTON. *(removes glasses, looks at them, muses)* It's years since I could find anything in one of *those*. *(the glasses restored, leans forward)* But you've not checked an Atlas?

ROSS. No...

PEMBERTON. Well, as it happens – Sligo is a county in Ireland. *(a question)* But you didn't know that.

ROSS. *(surprise)* No.

PEMBERTON. I suppose there must be some people named – or nicknamed – after it. *(a question)* But you'd never met anyone like that.

ROSS. Not to the best of my recollection, no.

PEMBERTON. Curious...really.

*(Although the lights remain up in **PEMBERTON**'s office, they also come up on **TAGGART** as he enters center area, drunk and scared.)*

TAGGART. Bless me, Father, for I have killed.

PEMBERTON. *(overlapping)* When I was younger – much younger –

TAGGART. *(overlapping)* But I haven't. Not yet.

PEMBERTON. *(overlapping)* We spent several summers in Ireland.

TAGGART. *(laughs)* Not the way I'm going to kill! *(pats his pockets without success, mutters)* Where's that bottle?

PEMBERTON. County Sligo, as it happens.

TAGGART. *(calls out)* Anita, my girl! Where are you?

PEMBERTON. But, of course, there's no way you could have known that. It's a nice –

TAGGART. ANITA – !

PEMBERTON. *(because* ROSS *has reacted sharply to* TAGGART*'s last cry)* David, are you listening to me?

(Although ROSS*'s attention has, in fact, become completely caught up in* TAGGART*, with* PEMBERTON *persisting, it swings back to him.)*

ROSS. Yes, doctor, of course.

PEMBERTON. It's a nice little puzzle, the number of coincidences between your dreams and reality. A little thing like a man ordering olives. A big thing like your wife being fantasized as your sister.

(He pauses, ROSS *says nothing.)*

You've been impotent since that dream?

ROSS. With my wife, yes.

PEMBERTON. There've been others?

ROSS. No. I mean, not here. Not in reality.

TAGGART. *(screams)* ANITA!

PEMBERTON. *(supplying the name from his notes)* Anita.

ROSS. Yes.

PEMBERTON. The prostitute –

ROSS. Yes.

PEMBERTON. Who is really – *(finds it in his notes)* your secretary.

ROSS. Yes! That's the point I'm trying to make. I don't think I'd be impotent with *her*.

PEMBERTON. I thought you proved that.

ROSS. I'm talking about here – in this reality. I've no question about it.

PEMBERTON. You say in *this* reality?

TAGGART. *(who has become aware of* ROSS *and* PEMBERTON*)* Careful!

ROSS. A slip of the tongue.

PEMBERTON. I see. *(makes a note)*

TAGGART. *(as* **ROSS** *leans forward to see)* What's he writing? Is he on to us?

> *(But* **PEMBERTON** *notices* **ROSS** *leaning in and adjusts the notepad so that* **ROSS** *cannot see it.)*

Damn!

PEMBERTON. *(as* **ROSS** *settles back)* You know, there's nothing necessarily wrong with having some doubts about reality. They occur to all men from time to time.

ROSS. Well, I –

TAGGART. *(interrupts)* Don't let him suck you in!

PEMBERTON. Of course, if the feeling becomes too pronounced...

TAGGART. What does he mean?

ROSS. What do you mean?

PEMBERTON. It's typical of a certain type to believe he's dreaming.

TAGGART. What type?

ROSS. What type?

PEMBERTON. Well...the homicidal maniac.

TAGGART. Oh, God!

PEMBERTON. Of course, that isn't *you*...

TAGGART. Then why bring it *up*, fatso?

PEMBERTON. The point is, the homicidal maniac can't kill otherwise. No one can kill who truly believes his victims are as real – as human – as he is.

TAGGART. *(enraged, begins to bridge the distance between himself and* **PEMBERTON***)* I'll kill *you*, you bastard!

> *(But* **ROSS** *is suddenly in his way, his back to* **TAGGART** *and arms spread wide, barring* **TAGGART***'s entrance into the office light frame.)*

ROSS. *(a cry from deep inside)* But this *is* real! *I* am real! *This* is real!

(**TAGGART** *backs away sharply, but continues to observe.*
ROSS, *emotionally drained, collapses into a chair.*)

PEMBERTON. *(studies* **ROSS** *carefully as* **ROSS** *recovers from the outburst)* Would you like a...cup of coffee?

ROSS. No...I'm all right.

PEMBERTON. *(searches his attaché case)* I've another sandwich here. You know I've been taking you during my supper hour, but I hate to sit here and make a pig of myself.

TAGGART. *(a gut scream)* PIGGG!!!

PEMBERTON. *(seeing* **ROSS** *'s reaction)* What is it?...Pig?...The Sligo connection. I see I'll have to watch my metaphors more closely.

ROSS. *(as he recovers)* Doctor, do you think...Could I be undergoing a nervous breakdown?

PEMBERTON. A layman's term. Let's just say...you're experiencing certain guilt feelings.

ROSS. From what I did in the Pepper case?

PEMBERTON. What did you do in the Pepper case?

ROSS. I told you...I got them off.

PEMBERTON. *(a calm denial)* No.

ROSS. I told you...I'd forgotten it, forgot all about it, but Charlie Bishop reminded me. They're a big pharmaceutical concern – pushing drugs here through dummy corporations in Mexico. Two years ago I got the indictment against them thrown out.

PEMBERTON. Well...that was your job, wasn't it?

ROSS. You're sure I didn't mention this to you?

PEMBERTON. I'm afraid you haven't.

ROSS. There's...another indictment against them. It'll be thrown out too.

PEMBERTON. I understand it's your duty to defend a client.

ROSS. My client was...is...I shouldn't say guilty, but that's what they are!

PEMBERTON. *Isn't* it your duty to defend them?

ROSS. There is evidence –

TAGGART. You're going too far, Dave.

PEMBERTON. What's that? I didn't hear you.

TAGGART. Don't say it!

PEMBERTON. What did you start to say?

ROSS. *(has actually forgotten, finds this most curious)* Nothing. I don't *know* what I was going to say.

PEMBERTON. Curious. This Pepper case interests me. Suppose we take it up at our next session?

ROSS. *(checks his watch)* Is it time?

PEMBERTON. I'm afraid so. *(finds sandwich he offered ROSS)* I'll finish *you* when I get home. *(puts it back in case)*

ROSS. *(nervous, uncertain)* Dr. Pemberton – will you renew my prescription?

PEMBERTON. *(preoccupied with his preparations)* The Seconal and so forth? No...you'll get by without them. *(suddenly checks his notes)* Did you say you defended that company two years ago? I note you started both your prescriptions then. Yes, we'll have to explore this Pepper thing further.

TAGGART. Get the pills!

ROSS. I...I don't want to dream tonight. If you'd just prescribe *something...*!

PEMBERTON. Afraid you'll kill Sligo?

ROSS. I don't know.

PEMBERTON. Or he'll kill you?

ROSS. He can't kill me. The dreamer never dies.

PEMBERTON. *(grins)* Ah, that old wives' tale – which happens to be true! The dreamer *does* never die – unless, of course, he dies in real life.

(ROSS reacts sharply, but PEMBERTON laughs.)

But I wouldn't concern myself with that. You're certainly sound of body.

(Hesitates, aware he has said too much by saying too little, makes a small, embarrassed shrug and steps out of light frame.)

ROSS. Dr. Pemberton –

PEMBERTON. *(off)* Just getting my coat.

ROSS. I…I may kill Sligo if I dream tonight.

PEMBERTON. *(off)* What if you do?

ROSS. I don't know.

PEMBERTON. *(off)* What if you slowly strangle him to death? *(re-enters, jovial, with coat over arm)* Sligo is the personification of all that's evil in you dream. If you kill him… maybe the dreams will stop.

*(***TAGGART***, having listened carefully to this last, suddenly bolts from the stage. The lights in his area drop at once. And ***PEMBERTON*** picks up the attaché case.)*

I hate analysis on the run – but I've a train to catch.

(He exits.)

ROSS. *(calls after him)* I'm not going to do it. I won't do it. I won't kill him! Do you hear me, Dr. Pemberton?

*(Lights slowly fall in the office and come up downstage center, muted traffic noises – the distant honking of horns, etc. – suggesting that the scene represents the street. But the traffic noises fade as ***SLIGO*** enters the frame, his hands jammed in his pockets as he looks warily up and down the "street.")*

SLIGO. No sign yet. *(checks his watch)* Well, we've a minute or two. The lad will show, I'm sure of it.

*(***BLACKMAN*** enters.)*

BLACKMAN. Good evening, Lieutenant Charlie.

SLIGO. Blackman! What do *you* want? *(His right hand raises slightly in his pocket.)*

BLACKMAN. You won't be needing that extra bulge, baby. Taggart chickened. He ain't coming.

SLIGO. To tell me that he sent the likes of you?

BLACKMAN. My good turn for the po-lice department. You ought to know better than anybody that I don't stay in business without cooperation. Keep cool, pig.

(begins to exit)

SLIGO. Hold a moment!

> *(His left hand is out of his pocket, on **BLACKMAN**'s shoulder. His right hand, however, remains in his pocket, obviously holding the gun.)*

BLACKMAN. *(perfectly still, his back to **SLIGO**)* You want something?

SLIGO. A little *more* cooperation if you please. Where did Taggart go? If he's skipped...

BLACKMAN. *(faces **SLIGO**, points to **SLIGO**'s right hand)* Baby, my mama always said it was impolite to point.

SLIGO. *(laughs, takes right hand out; the small pistol is in it)* You're afraid of this *toy?*

> *(Returns pistol confidently to pocket, both hands empty now, takes **BLACKMAN**'s shirtfront with left hand, threatens with his right.)*

Now, *Mister* Blackman, suppose you volunteer an answer or two?

> *(**TAGGART** appears behind **SLIGO**, a garrote stretched between his hands, waits his opportunity.)*

BLACKMAN. *(protests)* You're making it hard for me to breathe!

SLIGO. It's going to get a lot harder.

BLACKMAN. *(through clenched teeth)* You know it!

SLIGO. And what does *that* mean?

BLACKMAN. You'll find out, oinker.

SLIGO. Hey!

> *(This last is said as **TAGGART** is suddenly upon him, the garrote around **SLIGO**'s neck. **SLIGO** silently takes the cord with both hands and tries to kick backward at **TAGGART**.)*

TAGGART. Hold his legs, his legs.

> *(**BLACKMAN** falls to his knees, embracing **SLIGO**'s legs, pinning them together. The struggle continues as **SLIGO** tries to shake **TAGGART** off with his huge bulk.)*

TAGGART. …He's got his fingers in there!

BLACKMAN. *(also having a difficult time)* Squeeze, baby!

> *(***TAGGART*** *clearly redoubles his efforts.* ***SLIGO*** *'s right hand comes away from his neck, starts for his pocket.)*

BLACKMAN. The gun! He's going for the gun!

TAGGART. *(savagely) No!!*

> *(With a grunt and tug,* ***TAGGART*** *supremely increases his efforts.* ***SLIGO*** *'s right hand is halted on its way to his pocket. It starts up for the rope again.)*

SLIGO. *(unable to sustain the struggle any longer)* Mother of God!

> *(***SLIGO*** *'s right hand falls away from his neck, his great bulk toppling backward to the ground. For a moment* ***TAGGART*** *continues to kneel over him, his hands frozen to the rope. But* ***BLACKMAN*** *pushes* ***TAGGART*** *away.)*

BLACKMAN. Let him go! You'll saw his head off. *(finds a small object beside* ***SLIGO****)* What's this? *(Holds it up; it is a case for glasses.)* Who'd ever guess he wore glasses?

ROSS'S VOICE. *I* would.

> *(***TAGGART*** *reacts, looks about for the source of the* ***VOICE****, but* ***BLACKMAN*** *is already trying to move the body.)*

BLACKMAN. Come on – tote, baby.

TAGGART. What do we do?

BLACKMAN. *(easily)* We burn him.

TAGGART. *Burn* him?

BLACKMAN. You want fuzz coming around, asking questions, kicking you in the shins?

TAGGART. …No.

BLACKMAN. We burn him. *(having taken firm hold of* ***SLIGO*** *'s arm:)* Grab something!

> *(***TAGGART*** *gets himself under* ***SLIGO*** *'s left arm; they start out,* ***SLIGO*** *'s legs dragging.)*

Is this how you thought it would be, Special Forces? Is this the way you pictured killing the fat pig?

TAGGART. *(struggling with the weight)* …Sure.

BLACKMAN. *(laughs)* Feeling good, Charlie?

TAGGART. Feeling goddam good.

> *(As they exit, lights fall on street scene, rise in kitchen.* **FRAN** *dressed in a bathrobe, calls off and up.)*

FRAN. David, you'll be late.

ROSS. *(off)* Be right down, hon.

> *(She hums as she sets the table; it is apparent there is a different mood in this house.* **ROSS** *enters, the happiest we've seen him, checks his watch.)*

I *am* going to be late. Where's the paper?

FRAN. *(surprise)* You're not going to read it *now*.

ROSS. I *am* going to read it now. And I *am* going to be late. *(gives her a quick kiss as he reaches past her for the paper)* I may even take the morning off! I may invite you back upstairs to do that thing again.

FRAN. *(enjoying his mood too much to be really annoyed)* The girls will hear you.

ROSS. Let 'em. Why should they think sex is dirty, learning it in the streets? Let 'em think it's dirty at home.

FRAN. *(struggles to pull away)* David!

> *(But he gets another kiss and releases her.)*

If I knew Dr. Pemberton was going to do this good a job, I'd have sent you months ago.

ROSS. *(laughs)* It isn't just Dr. Pemberton. It's me, following Dr. Pemberton's advice. *(reading an article now)* …Had that dream again last night.

FRAN. *(stiffens slightly)* Did you?

ROSS. *(busy with his paper)* I killed a big fat cop named Sligo. You know what? I enjoyed it. *(turns to an inner page)*

FRAN. *(not certain how to respond)* Well, if that was Dr. Pemberton's advice…

ROSS. *(scan the inside page)* He not only advised it. He even suggested the technique. Strangulation.

FRAN. *(at a loss)* How very…therapeutic.

ROSS. What? *(glances up at her, laughs)* Yes, I guess… *(looks back at paper, his mood changing sharply)* Oh my.

FRAN. *(unaware of the change, tries to keep the kidding going)* I suppose there's something in wrapping your hands firmly around a windpipe that –

ROSS. *(interrupts, his voice low, hard)* Just-keep-quiet-for-a-minute. *(continues to read)*

FRAN. What is it?…David?

ROSS. *(puts paper down, looks up at her, frightened)* Strangulation. He was killed by strangulation.

FRAN. Who?

ROSS. Dr. Pemberton – last night. *(reads from paper)* "The distinguished psychiatrist apparently regurgitated some food shortly after going to sleep, a portion of it becoming lodged in his trachea…Mrs. Pemberton said he had eaten a late supper."

FRAN. That's terrible! *(Then, not unkindly, but only because her prime concern is **ROSS** – and she does want him to continue to improve:)* I guess you'll have to find somebody else.

ROSS. *(on his feet, enraged)* Find somebody else? Don't you understand? It was me! *I* killed him.

*(**FRAN** stares at **ROSS** in wonder and the beginning of horror. He meets her eyes for a moment and turns away. The lights go to black and the curtain falls on Act One.)*

ACT TWO

(Lights rise slowly on the **ROSS** *bedroom.* **ROSS** *sits on the edge of the bed smoking, lost in thought. After a moment,* **FRAN** *rises on one elbow.)*

FRAN. You'll have to sleep sometime, David.

ROSS. *(softly, more to himself than her)* Will I?

FRAN. It's almost a week. I don't think you've shut your eyes.

ROSS. But I have. I sleep on the train, back and forth to work. I don't dream. I keep expecting to, but I don't... dream.

FRAN. Is it over? Are the dreams behind us?

ROSS. I don't know. Pemberton said they would be, but... Pemberton's dead.

FRAN. Why not accept Jack's explanation? He checked with the radio station. It's entirely plausible.

ROSS. It's pat. Pat isn't plausible.

FRAN. It was on the news since midnight. Our clock radio went off at six twenty-five. You heard the six-thirty news.

ROSS. *(through gritted teeth)* I did *not* hear it.

FRAN. You heard it, but you don't remember. It became part of your dream. The alarm went off at twenty to seven. That's when you...officially...woke up. That's when you and I...

(She waits but he says nothing; she touches his hand.)

I'd like to do that thing again.

ROSS. *(withdraws his hand)* Let me be, will you? Go back to sleep.

FRAN. *(fighting anger)* It may surprise you, but you're not the only one who has trouble sleeping lately.

ROSS. Now what? You get angry? You scream at me? Is that what you're building up to?...Go ahead if it'll make you feel any better.

FRAN. *(tense, fighting it)* I may scream, but it will *not* make me feel any better! *(in control once more, sits beside him)* I'm sorry. I don't mean to make things any harder for you.

ROSS. ...I know, hon.

FRAN. You really *should* think about seeing another doctor.

ROSS. No.

FRAN. Can it hurt?

ROSS. *(looks at her)* Did it hurt Pemberton?

FRAN. David, you've got to do *something*.

(He does not reply. There is a pause.)

Can't you talk to *me?* Tell *me* about the problem. I'm no psychiatrist, but I'm a fair listener. You can't just keep it bottled up inside you.

ROSS. Do you know what I did today? I mailed a letter.

FRAN. *(trying to follow)* Did you?

ROSS. Yes, but I didn't sign it. They can't trace it back to me.

FRAN. *(confused)* Who can't?

ROSS. *(beat)* You wouldn't understand.

(A moment passes. Then:)

ROSS. Do you know...you remind me of my sister?

FRAN. *(more confused)* What sister?

ROSS. It's out of my dream, Fran. I didn't want to tell you.

FRAN. Why shouldn't you want to –

ROSS. Let me be blunter. You don't remind me of her, you *are* her, in my dream. That's why I – you and I – that's why we're having such a difficult time.

(He waits for her to comment; when she doesn't:)

You said you wanted me to talk to you. There it is.

(She impulsively kisses his cheek.)

ROSS. What's that for?

FRAN. *(innocent)* A sisterly kiss.

ROSS. *(angry)* Cut it out.

FRAN. I don't mean to joke. I kissed you because – All this time I thought – Well, I assumed the problem was –

ROSS. *(impatient)* What?

FRAN. In your dream – there was somebody else.

ROSS. *(not sure how to reply)* Oh?

FRAN. And I kept asking myself: How do I fight another woman if all you're doing is *dreaming* about her? Honest to God, I'm relieved.

ROSS. Are you?

FRAN. You're not the first man whose wife reminded him of his sister. We'll work it out, David.

ROSS. *(considers this, feels better)* You think so, huh?

FRAN. Yes.

(He turns to her, perhaps ready to start working it out right now. But as he turns, we hear:)

ANITA'S VOICE. You were talking in your sleep last night.

FRAN. *(as ROSS reacts to the VOICE)* What is it, David?

ROSS. Nothing.

ANITA'S VOICE. *(laughs)* You kept calling me Fran.

FRAN. *(who clearly does not hear the VOICE)* Your dream. Are you thinking about your dream?

ROSS. *(suffering)* No!

(ROSS compulsively reaches for a cigarette.)

FRAN. Fight it, David. If it *is* your dream, fight it.

ROSS. *(pulls away from her, agitated)* For God's sake, let me be!

(He puts the cigarette in his mouth and fumbles for matches.)

ANITA'S VOICE. Here…I'll light it for you.

(There is the flare of a match from **ANITA***'s bedroom. It cues her bedroom's lights to rise at once to full, and those in the* **ROSS** *bedroom to fall to black as quickly.* **ANITA***, wearing only a slip, and* **TAGGART***, fully dressed, are in positions similar to those of* **FRAN** *and* **ROSS***. She lights* **TAGGART***'s cigarette and blows the match out. He grins at her and we see in that grin subtle changes that have taken place since the murder. His jauntiness is somewhat forced; his teasing carries more than an edge of cruelty. For although the force of hate will not erupt in him until later in the scene, its seeds are present now.)*

TAGGART. *(comfortable, easy)* Had a little scare.

ANITA. *(interested)* Oh?

TAGGART. Damn near told her about you.

ANITA. *(surprise)* Really?

TAGGART. *(shrugs)* She was after me, curious, telling what a good listener she is, dying to find out. *(laughs)* Women like to come on that way.

ANITA. *(stares at him, entranced)* This is crazy, you know that?

TAGGART. Hmmm?

ANITA. You're standing here talking about some goddamn hallucination just like it's the real thing.

TAGGART. *(shrugs)* Maybe it *is*.

ANITA. You mean, maybe you're really married.

TAGGART. Maybe.

ANITA. *(challenging him)* This Fran dame, maybe *she's* real too.

TAGGART. Could *be*.

ANITA. *(anger)* And what the hell does that make me?

TAGGART. *(smug)* A figment of my imagination.

ANITA. *(disgusted, chooses and pronounces her word carefully)* Beans.

TAGGART. You might be, Anita. Pemberton thought you were.

ANITA. Am I supposed to know who that is?

TAGGART. A doctor I went to, a shrink.

ANITA. *You* went to him or *Ross* went to him?

TAGGART. *(shrugs)* What difference does it make?

ANITA. You're sick, Dave. You know that? You're flipped out of your skull.

TAGGART. Now you're taking Pemberton's side. In this world, according to him, I'm a homicidal maniac.

ANITA. *(angry, refusing to take him seriously)* Oh, cut it out.

TAGGART. I'm the only one, according to Pemberton, who actually exists here. I could snap your neck like that – *(snaps his fingers)* and never regret it.

ANITA. *(gutsy)* You'd regret it all right.

TAGGART. What makes you think so?

ANITA. You'd have to find somewhere else to sleep.

TAGGART. *(laughs)* You're right. You know that? You're right.

(As he continues to laugh, she shakes her head at his foolishness and splashes liquor into two glasses at the night table.)

ANITA. *(hands him a drink, his laughter subsiding)* Davey, let me ask you a question. Serious now.

TAGGART. *(humors her)* Sure. Serious.

ANITA. You ever *really* get confused? I mean, between what's dreams and what's real.

TAGGART. *(who would rather not answer)* You say "really"? Well...

ANITA. *I* do.

TAGGART. *(Not the most interesting thing he's ever heard.)* Oh yeah?

ANITA. Sometimes I think of things that happened to me when I was a kid – and then I remember they never *really* happened. I only dreamed them – or thought about them so much they *seemed* real. I'm going to be an old broad in a home someday, sitting in a rocking chair. And God, what stories I'll have to tell! Some of them will be true, some won't – and I bet I don't know the difference.

TAGGART. *(laughs)* That's a picture! You an old broad in a rocking chair.

ANITA. It's gonna happen. I know it. I mean, if I live that long. I dream about it all the time.

TAGGART. So I'm not the only one with screwy dreams.

ANITA. Course not. I don't know no one who don't dream. And believe me, one dream's as screwy as the next.

TAGGART. *(considers this)* Hmmm.

ANITA. *(gets comfortable next to him)* Did you ever get the feeling all of *life's* a dream? I mean, we're all asleep somewhere just thinking these things are happening?

(pauses for a moment)

You religious, Dave?

TAGGART. Any of your business?

ANITA. *I* was, when I was a kid. I wanted to be a nun. But we were Methodist. If you're Methodist, you can't be nun. I bet that surprises you.

TAGGART. What?

ANITA. Me being religious.

TAGGART. Nothing about you surprises me.

ANITA. *(takes it as a compliment)* Well, you're nice to say so. Anyway, I used to think what heaven really is – it's what happens when we wake up from this dream we're having. And death, you know, death is the alarm clock.

(Her clock goes off, giving both a start. She gets to it and shuts it off.)

Crap!

(then:)

You ever think anything like that?

TAGGART. What?

ANITA. What I just said!

TAGGART. *(muses)* Pemberton would have said so.

ANITA. *(uncomfortable)* Forget Pemberton, ha?

TAGGART. Pemberton would have said the only way *you* thought of it *I* thought of it first.

ANITA. Will you stop it now?

TAGGART. *(conciliatory, reaches for her)* Anita...

ANITA. *(pulls away)* I'm tired of it, Davey! This junk about everything being part of your dream. For all you know you're part of *my* dream. For all you know, *I'm* the dreamer, *you're* the goddam figment!

TAGGART. *(pursues her)* Listen, ha?

ANITA. *(turns on him)* Why *can't* this be my dream? Can you *prove* it ain't?

TAGGART. *(as he realizes he can indeed, takes her shoulders)* Listen.

(She stares up at him, frightened, and listening.)

I *can* prove it. I can prove it with *you* the way I did with Sligo.

ANITA. *(her curiosity getting the better of her fear)* What did you do with Sligo?

TAGGART. I killed him. Then I burned his body.

ANITA. *(who would pull away now)* You're nuts.

TAGGART. *(holding her)* Sure. So my killing you...doesn't count.

(His hands move down to her throat.)

ANITA. Hey!

TAGGART. The dreamer never dies, did you know that? Should I prove it, baby? Should I prove *I'm* the dreamer? Not you?

ANITA. *(a taloned hands swings at the upstage side of his face.)* I'll scratch your...

TAGGART. *(an injured grunt as his head jerks away from the talons)* Ugh!

*(As he did with **SLIGO**, he tightens his grip and she must forego her attempt to reach his eyes and return to his hands.)*

ANITA. Davey, don't!

TAGGART. Admit it, why don't you? Say I'm the dreamer. *Say* it, Anita!

ANITA. *(barely a whisper)* Davey...

TAGGART. *Say it!*

ANITA. Ohhh...

> *(Her head falls, her hands drop from his, her whole body sags into stillness on the bed.)*

TAGGART. *(suddenly frightened, takes her shoulder)* Hey, I was only kidding. I was kidding! Anita...?

> *(Her head suddenly snaps up, her voice weakened but coldly furious in victory.)*

ANITA. Ha! I *knew* you couldn't prove it.

> *(There is screaming from the other bedroom – and lights drop at once in ANITA's room and come there. But it isn't one scream we hear. It is two: FRAN's high cry-for-her-life and ROSS's immediate and then simultaneous, guttural but rising and sustained response—that is, a kind of maniacal and waking "Hah-ah-ahhhhhhh!" The two are in the same positions TAGGART and ANITA shared a moment ago, ROSS's hands tight on FRAN's throat. But she somehow tears herself away, leaving him to stare in horror at his hands.)*

FRAN. *(with no little difficulty)* What...are you trying...to do?

ROSS. *(in torment)* Oh my God.

FRAN. *(as she sees him clearly)* Your face! Look at your face!

> *(ROSS turns, touches what was the upstage side of his face, and we see the blood on his cheek and hand.)*

ROSS. There's got to be an answer...Somewhere there's an answer.

> *(Lights fall slowly in the ROSS bedroom and rise in the bar. TAGGART is alone, mean, drunk, and brooding over a bottle of Scotch. As he finishes a drink, he calls.)*

TAGGART. Julio! How about another – *(But he now sees he has the bottle.)* Screw it.

*(He pours himself a stiff one and drinks some of it. **PEPITO** enters and stands silently across the table from him.)*

TAGGART. Hell, what do *you* want?

PEPITO. To talk, David.

TAGGART. *(mimics his accent)* To talk, David. *(giggles and takes another swig)*

PEPITO. *(sits)* We must talk, my –

TAGGART. Cut it! I'm *not* your friend. Get the hell out of here,

PEPITO. *(persists)* I saw your sister. She is concerned about you. All of us are. At the Halfway House, we would like you to come back.

TAGGART. Screw the Halfway House. What do I care?

PEPITO. *(haltingly, with difficulty)* We have a brotherhood, David, in drugs. No man is alone, by himself –

TAGGART. *(mockingly)* Not a freaking island, eh?

PEPITO. *(protests)* When you hurt, we hurt.

TAGGART. GET OUT OF HERE!

PEPITO. *(unbudging)* David, *I* need you.

TAGGART. *(cold, quiet)* Split, greaser.

*(**PEPITO** stiffens and exits. After a moment **BLACKMAN** enters, sits beside **TAGGART**.)*

BLACKMAN. I got what you came for, Charlie. *(shows him a bankbook, opens it)* Fifty – five oh – big ones. Withdraw 'em when you need 'em. No questions, guaranteed.

*(**TAGGART** takes the bankbook with hardly a glance, slips it into a pocket.)*

You better start thinking, my man, about leaving town. *(when **TAGGART** makes no comment)* Hey, you listening?

TAGGART. *(drinks)* Sure. Why not?

BLACKMAN. I don't know what's going on in that honky mind of yours – or what you did to our little white sister – but she's blabbing all over town you bumped Sligo. Men with badges – big men with big badges – are going to be around looking for you. If they grab, they're like to grab me. It don't please me, Charlie.

TAGGART. *(looks at* **BLACKMAN** *for the first time)* What's out of town?

BLACKMAN. An introduction. Friends of mine. A job.

TAGGART. What kind of job?

BLACKMAN. One you're good at.

TAGGART. *(insists)* What kind of job?

BLACKMAN. *(laughs)* Cool it, my man. You'll find out.

TAGGART. Blackman, see these fingers?

BLACKMAN. Yeah –

(He barely gets the word out before **TAGGART** *'s other hand slaps him across the mouth and takes the front of his shirt, pulling him close.)*

TAGGART. *(easy)* I'll ask you one more time: What kind of job?

BLACKMAN. *(ice)* Charlie, you let go of me right now...or you're dead.

*(***TAGGART** *holds him a moment more as the tension between the two builds, then finally releases him.)*

TAGGART. *(silly, sobering rapidly, and scared)* Hell, what did I do *that* for?

BLACKMAN. I'm going to play a game with you. I'm going to play you're so damn drunk you don't know *what* you're doing. *(stands)* But never – I mean *never* – do that again. *(quietly)* You got me?

TAGGART. *(forces a laugh)* Yeah. Yeah, sure.

BLACKMAN. Nobody touches me.

(Exits quickly as **TAGGART** *stares at his hands. Lights fall in the bar and come up in the office.* **ROSS** *is at his desk, staring at his hands.* **BECKY** *enters wearing a coat and carrying a large handbag.)*

BECKY. Uh…excuse me.

ROSS. *(looks up at her surprised and confused)* Becky!…Is it quitting time?

BECKY. No – well, yes – it is – for me. *(takes a step back)* I've said good bye to everybody else. I didn't want to leave without saying good bye to you.

ROSS. I don't understand.

BECKY. *(sighs)* Well…it's been…interesting…working for you. I hope you'll give me a good reference.

ROSS. *(as it finally gets through to him)* You're…quitting? A better job?

BECKY. No job. Not yet. I'll find something. I have to go now.

ROSS. You haven't told me why you're leaving.

BECKY. I'm sorry, David – Great! Now I can call you David! – I don't think you'd understand.

ROSS. Try me.

BECKY. *(equivocal)* I'm not sure *I* understand.

ROSS. Come on.

BECKY. *(finally)* I don't know. I'm *scared,* that's all.

ROSS. Of what? ..*Me?*

BECKY. …Yes.

ROSS. Why?

BECKY. I don't know! Listen, I really have to – *(another step back)*

ROSS. But what did I *say?* What did I *do?*

BECKY. Nothing!

ROSS. *(tries to piece it together)* Then…?

BECKY. Don't expect it to make sense. It doesn't *make* any sense!

ROSS. If you'll just *tell* me…

BECKY. *(at last)* Beans. *(then:)* I dreamed about you. Beautiful, ha?

ROSS. *(stunned)* You *dreamed?*

BECKY. *(accusing)* You scared the pants off me! Darn it, you scared me half to death!

ROSS. But *how?* What did I *do?* Did I...hurt you?

BECKY. *Yes!* You hurt me!

ROSS. Did I choke you?

BECKY. *Yes!* You – *(breaks off, her anger replaced by fear; quietly)* How could you *know?*

ROSS. *(looks at her hard)* How could *you* know?

(She stands petrified a moment; then she suddenly cries out and exits. He makes no move to follow, the words of realization at last on his lips:)

But that couldn't be it...*could* it?

*(**CHARLIE** enters, clearly in a hurry.)*

CHARLIE. Excuse me a second, Dave. *(crosses to desk, gets brief)* I need this baby.

ROSS. Charlie! Have you got a minute?

CHARLIE. No way. I've got three men from Pepper in my office. Things are happening.

*(**CHARLIE** starts out.)*

ROSS. Give me a minute anyhow. Just one.

CHARLIE. *(sees he is disturbed)* What is it?

ROSS. *(proffers a chair)* Here, sit down...It's important, Charlie.

*(**CHARLIE** sits, glances at watch. **ROSS** brings his own chair around and sits so that they are in positions approximating those of **TAGGART** and **BLACKMAN** in the previous scene.)*

All right. Now...I want your full attention.

CHARLIE. *(under the pressure of time)* Dave...

ROSS. *(raises his hand)* See these fingers?

CHARLIE. *(recoils instinctively)* Hey!

ROSS. *(gratification)* You flinched!

CHARLIE. Huh?

ROSS. You flinched, Charlie. I didn't do anything. I only raised my hand. *Why did you flinch?*

CHARLIE. Dave, what kind of a game –

ROSS. This is important. Trust me. Why did you jump back just now? What came into your mind?

CHARLIE. *(looks at him uncertainly)* I don't know…Tell you the truth, I thought you were going to hit me.

ROSS. *(pounces on this) Why?*

CHARLIE. *(shrugs helplessly)* I don't have the faintest idea.

ROSS. Have I ever hit you?

CHARLIE. Hell no.

ROSS. And yet you thought…

CHARLIE. *(checks his watch)* Look, Dave, I've got to go. If you don't have a desperate need for me… *(rises)*

ROSS. *(turns away, in his own thoughts)* No, I'm straight.

(CHARLIE stares at ROSS's back without the first idea of what is going on in ROSS's mind, then starts out of the office.)

Oh, Charlie?

(CHARLIE pauses.)

How's the Pepper case coming?

CHARLIE. I told you. Things are happening. Jack Miles got his hand on some new evidence – the stuff I was asking *you* about. They got to someone his staff – but they can't get to *him.*

ROSS. *(carefully)* Where did he get this…evidence?

CHARLIE. Who knows? But my clients are going to jail. And I say… *(a happy whisper)* Hooray.

(CHARLIE exits.)

ROSS. *(grins, whispers quietly)* Hooray.

(Lights fade to black in the office and come up in the street. TAGGART, having set a small suitcase down, paces back and forth, checking his watch.)

TAGGART. *(under his breath)* Blackman, come on, come on.

(**MEREDITH** *enters. He does not see her.*)

MEREDITH. *(calls softly)* Davey?

TAGGART. *(surprise)* Fran? *(sees her)* Meredith!

MEREDITH. I was at the Halfway House, looking for you. I saw Pepito.

TAGGART. Mer, I can't talk to you now. There's trouble.

MEREDITH. That's why I'm here, Davey.

TAGGART. *(turns away)* I said I can't talk to you.

MEREDITH. *(goes to him, steadies her voice with difficulty)* It isn't very fair, you know. We've always been close, Davey – maybe too close. I've been more than a sister to you. I –

TAGGART. *(As she touches his shoulder, he whirls to face her.)* Will you get out of here?! Will you leave me alone?!

MEREDITH. I only want to help.

TAGGART. *You can't help!*

(His vehemence causes her to back a bit. She studies his face for a moment and then, giving up, withdraws an envelope from her purse.)

MEREDITH. Pepito gave me this...for you. *(puts it in his hand)* Good bye, Davey.

(She exits. He stares after her a minute, glances distractedly at the envelope and puts it in a pocket as **BLACKMAN** *enters, carrying an envelope of his own.)*

BLACKMAN. *(all business)* Got your airline ticket. *(hands it to* **TAGGART** *and produces a wallet)* Phony ID – ticket's in that name – and you can use it on the street if you happen to get stopped. *(hands him the wallet too)* Now... you got a gun?

TAGGART. *(checking the material* **BLACKMAN** *gave him)* Taped to the back of my dresser.

BLACKMAN. *(surprise)* Where? The Halfway House?

TAGGART. No...What am I saying? *Ross* has the gun.

BLACKMAN. *(The first he's heard of* **ROSS.**) *Who?*

TAGGART. Forget it. I never said it.

BLACKMAN. *(decides to proceed)* All right, my man. You'll find one in your hotel room. Under the mattress. Wait one hour – you'll get a phone call.

TAGGART. What's the money going to be like?

BLACKMAN. Like before. Twenty-five K. It'll be at the hotel when you get back.

TAGGART. Cash?

BLACKMAN. All small bills. Take it, take off. Disappear. Call me in a month. Maybe I'll have something else.

TAGGART. *(picks up suitcase)* OK.

BLACKMAN. You're a cool one, Charlie. I'm going to miss having you around.

TAGGART. I'll be around, Blackman, bye and bye.

*(**BLACKMAN** extends his hand palm up. **TAGGART** slaps his fingers and exits, **BLACKMAN** watching after him. Lights dim to black on the street scene, come up in **JACK MILES**' office. **JACK** is on the phone.)*

JACK. *(an impatient sigh)* Yes, I'll see him, Mary. Hold the narc brief a few minutes – all my calls too. Oh! Call *Mrs.* Ross. Tell her he's turned up.

*(He hangs up and rearranges some papers on his desk as **ROSS** enters. A hearty salute:)*

Dave!

ROSS. *(slightly wild-eyed, aware of it, trying to contain his nervous enthusiasm)* Jack! I may have the answer.

JACK. *(grins)* Sure, fella. Sit down.

ROSS. *(pulls a chair close to **JACK**, sits)* I'm talking about my dream – what we *thought* was my dream. I may have something figured out.

JACK. I'm happy to hear it. Fran called this morning. She was worried about you.

ROSS. *(leery)* Fran called *here?*

JACK. *(laughs)* You don't mind, do you?

ROSS. *(who does mind)* What did she say?

JACK. *(opaque)* Nothing. Nothing at all – except she was worried. I guess you left your office in kind of a hurry – and they called *her*.

ROSS. Listen. I'm going to need your help.

JACK. You've got it. Whatever I can do.

ROSS. A little of your time, we might be able to clear the whole thing up.

JACK. *(Folds his hands, grins, but his actual response is his own secret.)* I'm listening.

ROSS. Now this is going to surprise you. You won't believe it at first. But somewhere there may be a city – a fairly good-size city – where a policeman named Sligo, or maybe that's his *nickname,* suddenly disappeared.

JACK. *(the name ringing a bell)* Sligo? Isn't he the policeman in your dream?

ROSS. Hear me out, Jack – will you?

JACK. Go ahead.

ROSS. Now I wish I could tell you the name of the city but so far no one has mentioned it. And when I'm – when I'm *there* – I never think to ask because everyone just kind of *assumes* I know what it is – *(laughs nervously)* including me, I mean. *(wonders if he's made his point)* This isn't easy to explain.

JACK. *(glances at his watch)* I've got time. I'm listening to you.

ROSS. But there are other clues. Its climate is close to ours. It may be on the same meridian we're on! There's a tavern, downtown someplace, owned by a man named Blackman. And, yeah, there's a halfway house for ex-drug users. It's on Second Avenue – near the corner of Second and Grand! That might be the biggest clue of all, Jack. How many halfway houses can there *be* in these United States?

JACK. *(friendly, as in jest)* Would you believe I have absolutely no idea?

ROSS. But someone knows. Maybe someone in Washington.

JACK. *(doesn't follow)* So?

ROSS. Don't you see? If you'll check with people *you* know, if you'll call them *now* – maybe we can find out...in time.

JACK. In time for what, Dave?

ROSS. There's a man, David Taggart. Even now he may be waiting at the airport. He's going to fly out to kill somebody. He's got a twenty-five thousand dollar contract.

JACK. David Taggart. Isn't that the name you said they call *you?* In your dream?

ROSS. Yes, but that's when I thought I *was* dreaming. Before I found out.

JACK. Before you found out what?

ROSS. Listen, do we have to discuss this now? If you'll just make a couple of phone calls...

JACK. We *have* to discuss it. You're a lawyer, Dave. Convince me. Convince me to make those calls.

ROSS. I don't know where to start. It was the – the *reality* of the dreams that got to me at first. Everything seemed so logical – and not just the logic of a dream, one that disappears when you wake up – but a logic that proved out – a logic that made me suspect the reality of my *own* situation. For a time I thought *both* of my existences might me dreams – my life as David Taggart, my life as David Ross. But now I see: Neither is. Both are real. Somehow my life – and David Taggart's – have come together.

JACK. *(skeptical)* What are you saying...ESP?

ROSS. More than that. Much more. Don't ask me how...but we share the same experiences, see people the same way. Even our friends, those closest to us, have begun to share personalities. There *is* a universal soul, you know. We're – none of us – islands, but all part of the continent.

JACK. *(sarcastic)* Like Donne said?

ROSS. Like...*Pepito* said. What happens to David Taggart
    has become as important as what happens to me.
    David Taggart *is* me. Will you make that call?

JACK. *(with difficulty)* I can't.

ROSS. But –

JACK. For God's sake, listen. You're sick, can't you see that?

ROSS. *(quietly)* Schizophrenia?

JACK. A person creates another world – a fantasy existence
    – and justifies it as well as he can. I know it's hard
    for you, but if you were in *my* shoes, you'd see it in a
    minute.

ROSS. I *am* in someone else's and I see things you'll never
    understand. *(begins to leave)*

JACK. *(in an effort to stop him)* Dave –

ROSS. My time is running out. I've got to find Taggart and
    stop him.

    (Exits quickly. JACK *would follow, but the phone is ring-
    ing. Answers it impatiently.)*

JACK. *Yes?... (His tone softens as he recognizes the voice.)* Yes,
    Fran. I'm bringing him home.

    *(Lights simultaneously fall in office and rise in a dim
    hotel room.* TAGGART, *who has been lying in bed, sits
    up, grins and reaches for a cigarette.)*

TAGGART. Real, ha? So I'm real. Thanks, Ross. I wouldn't
    have figured it out all by myself. *(laughs, holds watch
    close to his face to check it in the dim light)* Almost time.
    What's this? *(finds an envelope)* Pepito's letter. *(He would
    crumple but, deciding instead to have a look:)* Oh hell.
    *(opens it, finds a single sheet of paper and, holding it close
    to see, reads aloud)* "David...I am entrusting this to your
    sister because by the time you read it I am sure I will
    be dead." *(leaps to his feet, furious) Damn,* Pepito! *(contin-
    ues with difficulty)* "I have not the strength of character
    to stay away from my habit now that I see what has
    happened to you."

PEPITO'S VOICE. *(as* **TAGGART** *continues to read silently)* "Perhaps I never had…strength of character. The pool table in our rec room…beneath the slate…I have long kept a certain envelope with certain things in it."

TAGGART. *(continues aloud)* "Today I went to it."

PEPITO'S VOICE. "I used it. And let me tell you I enjoyed it…too briefly."

TAGGART. "Tomorrow I'll OD."

PEPITO'S VOICE. "God help us both, David."

(The letter falls from **TAGGART***'s hand. He paces, filled with anxiety.)*

TAGGART. Now what? What do I *do*?

*(***TAGGART** *panics and cries out as a man would cry out to an unseen spirit.)*

Ross! Are you out there?…Ross! Can you hear me?… ROSS!! What do I *do*?

(There is a pause, then:)

ROSS'S VOICE. You follow through.

(Telephone rings, hard and insistent.)

TAGGART. *(slowly)* I…follow through. *(answers phone)* Yeah… Give me the name…*Him? (laughs)* Yeah, I know him. Where?…You're sure he's there?…No, I don't need directions. I could find my way blindfolded. *(hangs up)* The gun. *(searches under mattress, finds a pistol)* Yeah, the gun.

(Stares at it, contemplating. Lights fall in hotel room and come up in kitchen. **JACK** *sits at the table sipping a cup of coffee.* **FRAN** *enters.)*

FRAN. He's asleep now.

JACK. *(irony)* With anybody else I'd say that's a good thing.

FRAN. I called the number you gave me. They won't be able to come out till tomorrow morning. *(a sudden explosion)* I hate this, Jack. I really hate it!

JACK. He needs rest, Fran – and professional care.

FRAN. Christ, who knows *what* he needs?

JACK. *(goes to her)* Calm down.

FRAN. *(whirls on him, savage)* Don't *you* tell me that! The best friend lurking on the horizon. Always ready to step in if the going gets rough! Well, *I* need David – and the *girls* need David. You keep that straight, damn you.

JACK. *(angered at her unfairness, he would reply – but thinks better of it)* I'd better get back to my office.

(begins to exit)

FRAN. Jack…

(He stops, waits.)

Do I have to say it?

JACK. *(finally)* No.

(They are suddenly in each other's arms. They kiss gently, but with increasing passion. At last FRAN breaks it off and stares at him as if seeing him for the first time. She says it all with her eyes.)

(in reply) I know.

(ROSS enters in bathrobe.)

ROSS. I guess we all know now.

FRAN. *(moves away from JACK)* David!

JACK. Buddy, we were just –

ROSS. Forget it. Sit down, Jack.

(ROSS has lost the extreme nervousness of the last scene. He seems quite calm – perhaps too calm. As he raises his hand, however, we see he is holding a pistol. FRAN reacts with a start. ROSS waves her to join JACK.)

You too, hon.

FRAN. David –

ROSS. Sit…please.

(JACK and FRAN sit at the table. ROSS crosses room, looks off as if through a window.)

ROSS. He'll be coming soon. I guess it's best if the three of us are together.

JACK. *(carefully) Who'll* be coming soon, Dave?

ROSS. *(with a grin of superiority)* You wouldn't understand.

JACK. *(forces the words out)* Are you talking about Taggart?

ROSS. *(looks out window, muses)* Wish I knew where he was. He knows where *I* am. He knows I've got this gun. We'd better be careful.

JACK. *(as his eyes meet* **FRAN***'s)* Sure, careful.

ROSS. *(grins and relaxes, allowing us to see he is entirely in control of himself now)* Humor me all you like, Jack. I know you don't believe a word I'm saying.

JACK. *(braving it)* I'm a little confused, that's all. Why should Taggart be coming here?

ROSS. He has a contract. I told you.

JACK. He intends to kill one of us?

ROSS. He intends to kill…*you.*

FRAN. *(starts to rise)* David, don't you think –

ROSS. *(waves her down)* Just sit, Fran. It won't be long.

JACK. Why should Taggart want to kill *me?*

ROSS. The Pepper Pharmaceutical case. You're the man they have to get to.

JACK. *Why?*

ROSS. You've got the evidence. They know it. They even know where it is.

JACK. *No one* knows where it is.

ROSS. Taggart knows. You still have that pool table in your basement, don't you? *(grins as* **JACK** *reacts)* Do you deny it's where you've hidden the envelope? Beneath the slate? You and Pepito – ! Do you know you think alike?

JACK. *(uncomfortable)* Well, what *about* Pepito? Is someone going to kill *him?*

ROSS. He wrote me – me, Taggart, what's the difference? He said he was taking a drug overdose – and may be dying now. Or maybe I can save him. By saving *you.*

JACK. *(rises)* Listen, Dave –

ROSS. *(casually takes aim)* Sit, Jack.

JACK. And if I don't – what do you do? Shoot me?

ROSS. *(a step toward him)* I told you to sit.

JACK. Sure, that's the plan. But you're not as sharp as I thought you were.

ROSS. *(a warning)* Jack...

JACK. Because the truth of this situation – *the truth* – is there is no David Taggart. You're the man who intends to kill me. No David Taggart. Only you.

ROSS. That is not the truth!

JACK. Think about it, Dave. You're fantasizing, yes – but you haven't lost your powers of logic. What difference can it make who shoots me? I still wind up dead – if that's what you want, if that's what all of this is really all about.

ROSS. *(a step closer)* I'm warning you...

JACK. *(takes* **FRAN**'s *arm)* We're going to leave this room, Dave. We're going to call the police and tell them to come out and get you. If you really believe there's a David Taggart, you'll let us go. If not – so be it.

*(***JACK*** starts out, propelling* **FRAN** *before him.)*

FRAN. *(stops at edge of light, one last appeal)* David...?

JACK. Go on, Fran.

(She exits. **JACK** *swallows, starts to follow her. But* **ROSS** *levels the pistol at* **JACK**'s *back, the desperation in his voice causing* **JACK** *to freeze.)*

ROSS. *I'm trying to save you!*

JACK. *(waits, frightened, though his voice is under steel control)* Do you shoot me or not?

ROSS. *(at last)* I can't.

(His pistol hand swings down as **JACK** *breathes a sigh of relief.* **JACK** *would start off again but* **TAGGART** *suddenly enters the scene from the opposite end of the stage, his pistol ready.)*

TAGGART. *I* can.

> (**JACK** *whirls to face him, but* **TAGGART** *is already firing, the shot pinking* **JACK**'s *left arm.* **JACK** *falls into a semi-sitting position, incredulous, holding the arm and staring at* **TAGGART**. **ROSS** *quickly crosses to* **JACK**'s *side, thus momentarily screening him from* **TAGGART**, *and, on seeing* **JACK** *is only wounded, turns slowly to face* **TAGGART**, *who has remained at the opposite end of the stage. The pistols are at both men's sides.*)

TAGGART. *(His voice even, familiar.)* Get out of the way, Davey.

ROSS. *(in what he senses will be his final decision)* ...No.

> (*Slowly the two men raise their pistols to full arm's length, taking deadly dueler's aim. As they aim, we hear a ticking clock, softly at first, but growing louder and louder until it fills the theater. Over the clock we hear the offstage voice of* **FRAN** – *or is it* **MEREDITH**? – *as she says, calmly at first, "Wake up, David." And then, with concern, "Wake up, David." And then, as she realizes the terrible truth, a piercing scream: "DAVID!!!" Immediately following her scream, the two men fire. Simultaneous with the explosion of their pistols is the vibrant ringing of an alarm, which continues as all time stops.* **JACK** *numbly clutching his arm,* **ROSS** *and* **TAGGART** *with pistols raised* – *all remain frozen as the lights slowly fall to black, the alarm ceases, and the final curtain falls.*)

PROPERTY LIST

ACT I

At times action flows from one space to the next without actual scene breaks. This necessitates some minor set changes done quickly & quietly in dark.

Preset:

Ross bedroom:

Double bed, night table & lamp
Rollerskates at bedside

Second bedroom:

Bed, nondescript quilt indicating room is Meredith's

Office space:

Desk, telephone, intercom, two chairs which, by re-angling the furniture, will denote three different offices.
Legal brief
Phone call message slips
Cigarette pack & matches/lighter & ash tray

Ross kitchen:

Table, chairs and perhaps a background of cabinets

Empty area:

Used for the pure "nightmare" of the opening scene & for the street scene later on.

Bar scene: largely a table, two chairs, two steins of beer

Carried off by:

FRAN:

Rollerskates

PEPITO:

Paper back book in pocket

BECKY:

Enters office with large styrofoam cup of coffee
Reenters with paper towels a short time later

PEPITO:

Paper back book

ANITA:

Takes Taggert's stein when exiting
Reenters with second stein of beer for Taggert
Enters with 2 glasses of scotch
Reenters with bottle of scotch

Carried on by:
ROSS:
> Bottle of olives
> Plate for olives

Changed in the dark by stage crew:
> Anita's bedroom:
> Night table is added, bed is re-angled, quilt is removed to reveal a lavender sheet.

Carried on by:
TAGGERT:
> Note to be pinned to pillow later in scene

Carried on by:
SLIGO:
> Small pistol…drop gun in his pocket
> Larger pistol…a .38 in another pocket

Desk & chairs rearranged by stage crew in the dark:

Carried on by:
BEMBERTON:
> Half-sandwich in hand & a whole one in attache case
> Notebook & pen
> Wearing reading glasses
> Attache case

Carried on by:
TAGGERT:
> Bottle of whisky

Carried on by stage crew in dark:
> Street scene: Lamppost

Carried on by:
SLIGO:
> Small gun in pocket

Carried on by:
TAGGERT:
> Garrote type rope

Carried on by:
BLACKMAN:
> Glass case

Carried on by:
FRAN:
> Breakfast dishes
> Morning newspaper

ACT II

Preset:

    Ross bedroom:

        Cigarette pack & matches/lighter & ashtray

    Anita's bedroom:

        Cigarette pack & matches/lighter & ash tray
        Two glasses & whiskey bottle
        Alarm clock

    Office space:

        Ross's desk, telephone, intercom, two chairs, brief, loose papers

    Ross kitchen:

        Coffee cup

    Bar:

        Two glasses & whiskey bottle

    Street scene:

        Lamppost

Carried off by:

TAGGERT & ANITA:

        Cigarette pack & matches/lighter & ash tray
        Two glasses & whiskey bottle
        Alarm clock

Carried in by:

BLACKMAN:

    Bank book

Carried off by:

TAGGERT:

    Two glasses & whiskey bottle

Carried on by:

BECKY:

    Large handbag

Carried on by:

TAGGERT:

    Small suitcase

MEREDITH:

    Purse & envelope

BLACKMAN:

    Envelope & wallet

Carried off by:
TAGGERT:
Suitcase, envelope & wallet

Changed by stage crew in dark:
Jack Miles office (reconfigure desk & chairs)

Changed by stage crew in dark:
Telephone is added to the night table and sheet is covered by a rough wool blanket to convert Anita's bedroom to a cheap hotel room. Cigarette pack on night table
Envelope with single sheet of paper in it on night table
Pistol under the mattress

Carried in by:
ROSS:
Pistol

Carried in by:
TAGGERT:
Pistol

SOUND EFFECTS

Police siren, police whistles, ringing phone, ringing alarm clock, muted traffic sounds, loud ticking clock, gun shots.

COSTUME PLOT

All modern day clothing...appropriate attire for story circumstances, ie. business clothing, party wear, street-clothes, waitress uniform, police uniform, underslip, nightgown, bathrobe, silk robe, woman's cheap cloth coat, woman's stylish coat, man's overcoat, wrist watches.

SET DESIGN FOR "DREAMS"

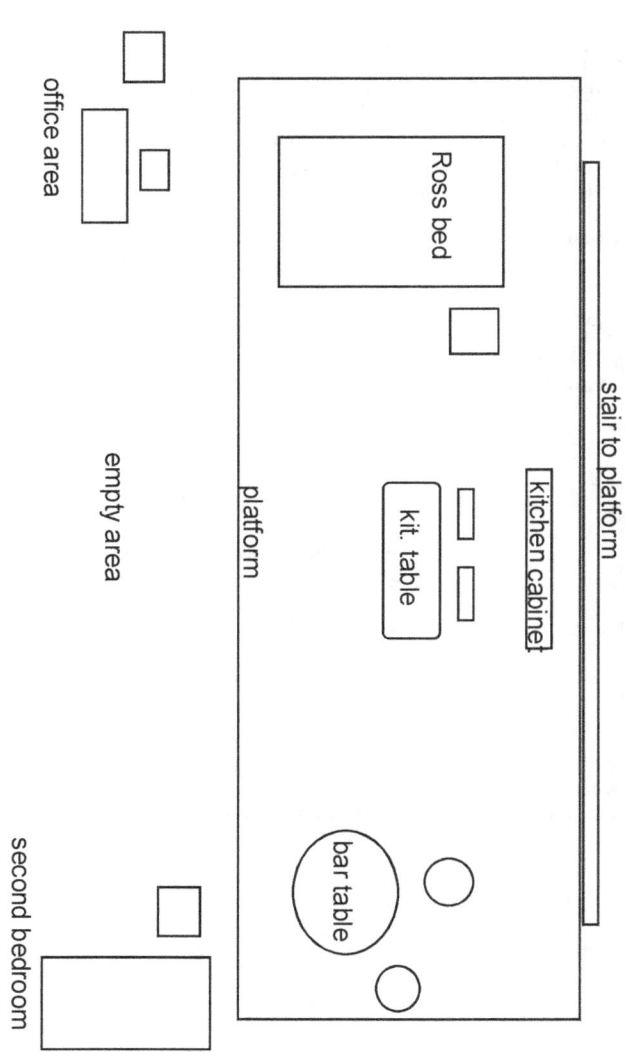

See what people are saying about
DREAMS...

Also by
Tom Sharkey...

Amy's Wish

Together Again

Just Say Yes!
(written with Jack Sharkey)

OTHER TITLES AVAILABLE FROM SAMUEL FRENCH

AMY'S WISH

Tom Sharkey

Comedy / 3m, 3f / Interior

Recently retired and newlywed, Sam Galway is flabbergasted when the spring water at his honeymoon retreat transforms dear old Amy into a 19-year-old knockout. His "young" bride attracts a youthful admirer while the sheriff becomes convinced that Sam has murdered Amy.

This romantic comedy by the librettist-composer of *It's a Wonderful Life*, the author of *My Heart Reminds Me* and the co-author of *Just Say Yes!* is a charming audience-pleaser.

> "A romantic comedy the entire family will enjoy!"
> – Howard Cobbs of the Gaslight Dinner Theatre